STAR
BABY

Hollywood Daughters

A Family Trilogy

STAR BABY

Joan Lowery Nixon

BANTAM BOOKS
NEW YORK · TORONTO · LONDON · SYDNEY · AUCKLAND

STAR BABY

A Bantam Book / November 1989

Produced by Daniel Weiss Associates, Inc.,
27 West 20th Street, New York, NY 10011.

The Starfire logo is a registered trademark of Bantam Books,
a division of Bantam Doubleday Dell Publishing Group, Inc.
Registered in U.S. Patent and Trademark Office and elsewhere.

Book design by Richard Oriolo

Library of Congress Cataloging-in-Publication Data

Nixon, Joan Lowery.
 Star baby.

 (Hollywood daughters: a family trilogy) (A Bantam starfire
hardcover book)
 Summary: Despite her interfering stage mother,
seventeen-year-old Abby, a former child movie star,
pursues her dream of becoming an actress in Hollywood
during World War II.
 [1. Actors and actresses—Fiction.   2. Mothers and
daughters—Fiction.   3. Hollywood (Los Angeles, Calif.)
—Fiction]   I. Title.   II. Nixon, Joan Lowery.
Hollywood daughters.
PZ7.N65Su   1989   [Fic]   89-15001
ISBN 0-553-05838-X

Published simultaneously in the United States and Canada

Bantam Books are published by Bantam Books, a division of Bantam Doubleday
Dell Publishing Group, Inc. Its trademark, consisting of the words "Bantam
Books" and the portrayal of a rooster, is Registered in U.S. Patent and
Trademark Office and in other countries. Marca Registrada. Bantam Books,
666 Fifth Avenue, New York, New York 10103.

PRINTED IN THE UNITED STATES OF AMERICA

FG   0 9 8 7 6 5 4 3 2 1

*For Mary Lou Bodnar,
who shares so many memories
of our teenaged, Hollywood years*

STAR
BABY

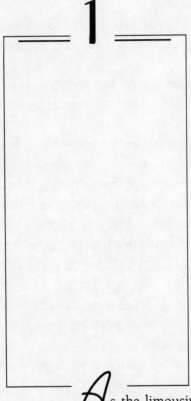

1

*A*s the limousine inched toward the curb in front of Grauman's Chinese Theatre, Abby Baynes grimaced and scrunched back against the upholstery.

Her mother nervously patted imaginary stray wisps of her blond hair into place, scooted to the edge of her seat, and bent to peer from the limousine window. "*Everybody's* going to be here! Absolutely everybody who's important!" she trilled, and turned to pat Abby's knee. "And look at all the fans who've turned out. They're here to see *you*, Cookie!"

"Mama, they're here for the premiere," Abby murmured. "They came to see the stars of the movie. I'm not even in it."

Her mother tossed her an impatient glance. "Don't be silly," she said. "The fans want to see *all* the stars, and that includes you."

With a jolt that almost bounced Abby's mother from her perch, the limousine stopped. The driver leaped out and hurried to the curbside door, opening it with ceremony.

Abby had to stoop to keep from bumping her head as she left the limousine. She stepped awkwardly onto the red carpet that stretched from the theater doors to the street. Her little-girl, black-patent-leather shoes pinched her toes, and her pink rayon taffeta dress, complete with broad sash and puffed sleeves, stretched tightly over her chest, painfully flattening her breasts and cutting into the flesh under her arms.

To Abby's left, large klieg lights hummed. Their mechanisms ground noisily as they swept against the low cloud cover that hung over Los Angeles, heralding one more extravagant movie premiere. Screeching, yelling, waving autograph books and pens, the crowd pressed against the ropes at each side of the courtyard. Countless pairs of greedy eyes ogled the arriving celebrities.

"He looked right at me! Did you see that? I think I'm going to faint!" The voice screamed so close to Abby's ear that she winced.

"Smile, Sweetie! Those are your fans!" Mama, fragrant with Chanel No. 5, gave Abby a little push toward the crowd while firmly gripping her elbow.

Abby twinkled obediently, turning on the adorable, dimpled, little-girl smile that had once brought people rushing to the box office to see *Our Girl, Taps on Parade,* and *Little Darlin'.*

The crowd tried unsuccessfully to shove forward. "There's Bob Hope! Lucille Ball! Oooh! Look at that mink coat!" Their squeals raked up Abby's backbone like fingernails on a blackboard.

With nervous steps she moved toward the ropes that restrained the yelling crowd. Her pasted-on, lighted smile blinked, then disappeared as she came face to face with one of the horde. The pudgy woman's eyes bulged with excitement, and her mouth worked like a fish, producing little bubbles of saliva at the corners. Their eyes met. For a moment the woman stared, then gasped in recognition.

"Hey!" she burbled. "Hey, I know you! Didn't you used to be Cookie Baynes?"

With a groan Abby turned away, muttering under her breath, "I *am* Cookie Baynes! I *am*! I *am*!"

At seven she had been the tiny child star with the pixie face who was called "Cookie." She'd made a salary most adult actors envied. But Abby was no longer the public's favorite child. She hadn't made a movie since 1937, with the exception of two box-office flops when she was in her early teens. Abby shuddered every time she thought about those. Now, in 1942, she was seventeen, tall and gawky, not yet an adult but too old for child parts. *If only Mama would admit it,* Abby thought. *Mama—*

A syrupy voice broke into her thoughts. "Why, it's Cookie Baynes. What a surprise to see *you* here."

Abby whirled to face Linda Larkin, whose wavy dark hair was dramatically accented by clouds of sparkling white net and sequins. Linda met Abby's surprised look with a grin. "Little Cookie Baynes," she purred. "My, my, haven't you grown."

"Cut it out, Linda." Johnny Erwin—tall and slender—stepped from Linda's side to give Abby a hug. "As you can see, the studio paired me with sweet-tempered Linda again," he murmured in Abby's ear.

"You think you've got it bad," she whispered. "Look who *my* date is—my mother!"

As the two of them laughed, Linda snapped, "What's so funny?"

"The picture, I hope," Abby said. "That's what MGM is counting on."

Abby's mother appeared beside her and planted a loud kiss on Johnny's cheek. "Johnny dear," she gushed, "where have you been keeping yourself? Why don't you come over some time to see Cookie? You used to be such good friends when you were making movies together."

With a sharp glance toward Abby, Linda spoke before Johnny had a chance to answer. "The studio keeps us both much, much too busy."

Abby's mother's smile was taut. "How nice for you," she muttered to Linda. Without waiting for a

4

response, she grabbed Abby's arm and pulled her toward the theater.

Abby was glad when the houselights finally faded and the picture began.

She tried to concentrate on the story, but she couldn't get that awful woman's words out of her mind: "Didn't you *used to be* Cookie Baynes?"

Abby had been a star, and she'd enjoyed being the center of a sea of smiling faces. "She's adorable," people had said. "She's talented. She's put the studio on the map."

Mama had known from the beginning that Abby would be a success. She'd taken her from studio to studio, determined to get Abby the opportunity she deserved. When an up-and-coming young studio had signed her, Mama had worked tirelessly to manage Abby's career. Ignoring the complaints and grumblings about her forceful methods, Mama had made sure that everybody, from gossip columnists to studio heads, gave Abby the full star treatment. Dad, who deferred to Mom about all matters concerning Abby, had beamed through his daughter's films and had praised her.

Oh, there were parts about being a star that weren't much fun, like having to wake up before it was light in order to get to the studio on time; and playing scenes over and over and over again when one of the other actors blew a line or the director wanted a different angle; and not being allowed to go outside until the script for the next day's scenes had been learned. But the praise, the attention, and the adulation that made

Abby feel so special was worth anything she had to do to get it.

She had been too young to think ahead, to imagine ever growing up and growing right out of her career. But suddenly, directors weren't looking for "cute" or "spunky" any longer. They were casting girls with well-rounded hips and breasts and faces glamorous enough for the covers of *Photoplay* and *Modern Screen*. The people who had told Abby she was wonderful disappeared from her life. She rarely was called for a part, and she finally was informed that the studio wouldn't renew her contract. The best her agent could do for her was to send her on an occasional circuit of noisy, smoke-filled banquet rooms, Rotarian luncheons and dinners for aging members of the D.A.R., where she performed the crowd-pleasing songs from her childhood.

On stage Abby would try to blot from her mind memories of the days in which she'd been treated as someone special, a child star. Fighting embarrassment, she'd sing in a high, clear voice before grandmothers who wiped sentimental tears from their eyes, waiters who slammed dirty dishes on their trays during her act, and people who were too drunk and noisy to listen.

After each performance her mother would pocket the envelope with the check inside and gurgle at Abby, "They love you, Sweetie."

In between gigs on the dusty, prickly-plush coach seats of trains that rocked and swayed and carried them to the next stop, Mama could be loving and funny. She'd tell Abby over and over again some of the stories from her childhood years, which were spent on the vaudeville stage with her song-and-dance-team parents. Lulled by the pleasing, familiar rhythm of Mama's voice, Abby would fall asleep with her head on her mother's shoulder.

But if Abby dared to complain about the rude audiences or the horrible embarrassment of trying to be a child when she wasn't, her mother's eyes would narrow with anger. "You wouldn't have a career without my sacrifices," she'd snap. "You wouldn't be America's favorite little girl if I hadn't given up my own career and dedicated my life to you. How can you be so ungrateful? Why can't you appreciate all I've done for you?"

Abby knew her mother's list of grievances as well as she knew the vaudeville stories. Eventually, the accusations would end. After a little more time, Mama would begin to unbend. She'd fumble through her purse for a tissue, mop at her blue-shadowed eyes, and blow her nose. She'd even try a wobbly smile. "So what if there aren't any movie roles for you right now, Sweetie? We're keeping your name and face before the public. That's what counts. Who knows who might be out there watching? The offers for film roles will be coming in again soon, and you'll be able to thank me for that, too." But she never, ever agreed to let Abby dispense once and for all with the dress or the shoes or the songs that had made little Cookie Baynes a star.

The houselights in the movie theater came on with a suddenness that caused Abby to squint.

Mama lowered her voice and murmured, "The picture was a flop. They're going to lose a bundle on this one. They made a huge mistake by casting you-know-who. Did you see the lines in her face? The best camera-man in the world can't hide those any longer."

When they arrived home, Dad met them at the door. "Well, well," he said, "did the two of you have fun?"

"Fun?" Mama repeated, shutting the front door behind them. "We didn't go to the premiere to have fun. It was business. It was having Abby seen by her fans and by all the right people."

Abby read the embarrassment in her father's eyes. She quickly stepped between her parents. Pretending to hold a microphone, she announced in a pompous voice, "Here we are, ladies and gentlemen, at Grauman's Chinese Theatre, preparing to meet all the right people. And here comes one of them now . . . the glamorous Gloria Gotalot. How did you happen to become one of Hollywood's right people, Gloria?"

Abby puffed out her chest, threw a hand on one hip, and said in a slow drawl, "I had two very good reasons, darling. Talent had nothing to do with it."

Dad laughed loudly, but Mama scoffed, "That isn't funny, Abby. It's vulgar." She opened a polished, inlaid cabinet, pulled out a decanter and glass, and poured a drink.

Abby's father's good humor vanished as he asked, "Isn't it a little late for that, Gladys?"

Mama took a swallow of the drink before she turned to face him, her eyes hard. "Last time you said, 'Isn't it a little *early*, Gladys?' Now you're asking if it isn't a little late. Make up your mind, dear." She took another, longer swallow.

"Drinking isn't the answer," he said.

"Answer to what?" she retorted. "I work so hard for Abby, and neither of you takes it seriously. You make fun of what I do—"

"Oh, no, Mama!" Abby interrupted. "I wasn't trying to make fun of you or the premiere. I was just—"

But her mother wasn't listening. This time, her anger was directed at Abby's father. "Why is it that for everything I try to do, I get an argument from you? I deserve a little relaxation, a little fun at least." Her voice became shrill as she slammed her glass down on the top of the cabinet and poured a second drink. "That could have been *me* up there on the screen tonight, but I gave up my career for this family."

Abby quickly slipped from the room and ran upstairs to her bedroom. She didn't need to listen to her parents' argument to know how it would go. "If only I hadn't married you!" Mama would scream at Dad. "If only I hadn't gotten pregnant!"

Although her mother's theater background consisted of nothing more than appearing as a third member of her parents' unsuccessful vaudeville song-and-dance team, Mama had glamorized the past in her memory. Abby was certain she didn't even recall the truth anymore.

On her eighteenth birthday Abby's mother had come to Hollywood. She'd been sure that a producer would discover her, sure that someday she'd be a star, as though "The Hoofing Howells" had been a Broadway hit. But she'd never landed a real role and had been working as an extra in a western film when she met Frank Baynes, a bookkeeper who lived in the same apartment house. Lonely and frustrated because her dreams hadn't come true, she had married Frank. They'd moved into a little court apartment on Fountain Avenue. Ten months later Abby was born.

In the dark bedroom Abby dropped her clothes on the floor, pulled a cotton nightgown over her head, and walked to the open window. Brushing strands of her long, straight brown hair from her eyes, she knelt at the window, resting her arms on the sill. She gazed down the hill past Laughlin Park Drive to the lights on Hollywood Boulevard. With the premiere over, the klieg lights were out. There'd been talk of banning the lights while the country was at war, but the studios still hadn't agreed the ban was necessary.

The sky was clear, and the high moon outlined each shadow in silver light. A too-sweet, heady perfume arose from the blooming jacaranda tree under the window; and in the distance there was the faint sound of traffic, an ambulance siren's wail, and a dog's halfhearted, answering bark.

As her parents' voices rumbled toward the entry hall, Abby climbed into bed, tugging the sheet and blanket up to her chin. The moon had risen higher now, and it shone through the open east window, adding a silvery sheen to the ruffled sheer curtains and the ruffles on Abby's canopy bed and on the skirt of her dressing table. In daylight the walls and fabrics in her room were a light, dainty pink—the same ones once featured in *Modern Screen* and copied by mothers of little girls all over the country. But at night the color faded into gray, and the yards and yards of ruffles became ghostly banners.

Abby heard her mother climb the stairs then pause outside the door of her room.

The doorknob turned slowly, and her mother stumbled in. "You're awake, aren't you, Cookie?" Mama asked.

"Yes," Abby murmured.

Mama plopped down on the edge of Abby's bed. She sniffed, as though she'd been crying, and reached for Abby's hand. In the soft moonlight, she looked gentle and vulnerable—as beautiful as Abby knew she once had been.

"Cookie, baby," she said, brushing a stray hair from Abby's forehead, "I was just thinking about your first audition." Mama smiled wistfully. "You weren't quite three years old, but you already knew how to read, and you remembered every little poem you ever heard. I had you in a pink dress with so many ruffles that the skirt stuck straight out, and your little white panties showed.

"I took you into the room where all these other mothers and little girls were waiting to be called. A woman sat at a desk with a large notepad and pencil. 'What's your child's name?' she asked me. You were such a smart, funny little cookie, with your bouncy curls and that pixie face that crinkled up and made everybody laugh. Suddenly the name 'Cookie' just popped into my head, and I said, 'Cookie Baynes. That's her name. Just watch. Pretty soon everyone in the United States is going to know that name.' And I was right." Gladys let out a long sigh. "Oh, those were good days. We were *somebody* in this town then."

"I remember," Abby said.

But Mama wasn't finished. "You wouldn't have been a star if it weren't for me," she went on, and a tear rolled down her cheek. "I could have been a star, myself, you know. I was young and beautiful." She patted at her hair, which was rolled and bobby-pinned in front, but swung free in the back. A more confident smile flickered across her lips. "I'm still beautiful. Isn't that right, Cookie?"

"Yes, Mama," Abby whispered, closing her eyes against the painful knot forming in her chest.

"No one would ever guess I'm old enough to have a daughter in her teens." Mama quickly added, "*Barely* in her teens."

"I'm not *barely* in my teens," Abby muttered, knowing that Mama was beyond hearing anything she said. "I'm seventeen."

"I was so sure my baby girl would be beautiful, too. Like me," Mama went on dreamily. "Instead, somehow I got this funny-faced little kid with a button nose."

"I'm sorry, Mama," Abby murmured. She could hear the tears in her own voice.

"Maybe it worked out for the best," Mama said. "You could make everybody laugh and cry, Cookie. They took you right to their hearts." There was a long pause. Then she added, "It's different now. There are a million kids your age out there hoping for studio contracts. If only . . . if only you were pretty."

Abby flinched, hunching her shoulders against the guilt that rushed over and around her. What had she done to make this happen?

Her years as a star had been a long series of pleasant, problem-free days. "You make your fans happy, Cookie," Mama had told her over and over again, "and you make Mama and Daddy happy, too—especially when you're a good girl and learn your lines and do everything the director tells you." It had been very simple.

But when had it ended? Abby remembered when she first began to realize that her parents were no longer happy. In spite of her constant striving to be a good girl, everything was going wrong. Cookie had suddenly become long-legged, her mouth was a little too wide, and her hair was a little too straight. The word "cute" didn't fit at all anymore. It was bad enough when her studio contract wasn't renewed; it became worse when she wasn't even offered bit parts.

All she had left were those degrading club performances. Mama insisted she take them to keep her name before the public. Eventually, Mama was convinced, they'd demand a Cookie Baynes comeback from the studios.

Abby wanted so much to please her parents. They'd been so proud of her. Mama had sacrificed so much for her career. More than anything in the world, though, she loved performing, loved being a star. She wasn't gorgeous, like Linda Larkin, but she knew she was a good actress. If only someone would give her a chance to prove it!

Trying to remain a child wasn't doing her or her

career any good at all. It made her feel ridiculous. But what if she refused? Maybe Mama was right. Maybe the smiling, bubbling little girl was all people really wanted from Cookie Baynes.

Abby shivered, and it wasn't from the night air.

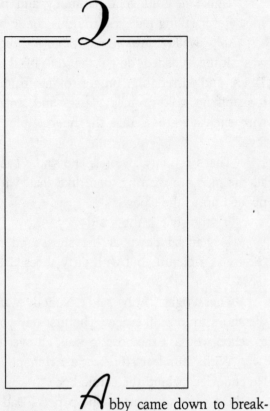

2

*A*bby came down to breakfast the next morning to find her father and her younger brother, Bobby, already sitting at the table. Bobby looked up and grinned. Then he stuck his face back inside a comic book, and shoveled spoonfuls of cornflakes into his mouth, smacking loudly.

He's the beautiful one, Abby thought. *And it's not fair. Boys don't have to be beautiful.* Hating herself for this instant of jealousy, she quickly bent to kiss Bobby on the forehead.

"Ugh!" he said good-naturedly and rubbed at the spot, never taking his eyes from his comic book.

Abby walked around the table to where her father was sitting, pushed down the top of the *Los Angeles Times*, and kissed him on top of his balding head. He took off his gold-rimmed glasses and smiled up at her with such sweetness that she hugged him in a rush of love.

"That's a pretty sweater," he said. "I've noticed that all the girls are wearing them like that, with the sleeves pushed up to the elbows."

"It's the style," Abby said.

He glanced down at her shoes and smiled again. "Pretty as a picture, but with dirty shoes. That's the style, too?"

"That's right," Abby said. "Nobody wants their saddle shoes to look like new. The first day you wear them to school you ask the boys to walk all over them."

"With your feet still in them, I hope," Bobby said. He chuckled behind the comic book.

"Do you want part of the paper?" Dad asked Abby. He held out the sections piled on the table at his left.

March 18, 1942. With a shiver Abby glanced at the front page: MacArthur named Allied Supreme Commander in the Pacific. Wartime draft lottery begins. Bombings in England. Axis submarines sink three ships. Bill to establish a Women's Army Auxiliary Corps passes the House.

"No, thanks," she told her father. "I'm running late. I'm just going to make some toast and eat fast."

Coralee, the Baynes's housekeeper, pushed open the swinging door between the breakfast room and kitchen. Her faded sandy hair was wrapped in an unkempt bun at the back of her neck and a large, white cotton apron was tied around her ample waistline. "Whatcha wanna eat?" she asked Abby.

"Thanks, but I just want toast. I'll take care of it," Abby said. She squeezed past Coralee to get into the kitchen. It could take Coralee forever to make a couple of slices of toast. It was hard enough for her to wake up enough to make the morning coffee.

"No wonder you're so skinny," Coralee said. "If you wanna fill out like the other girls, you're gonna have to eat more." She yawned, mouth wide, then turned to Abby's father. "Mr. Baynes, I'm fixin' to quit workin' for you folks pretty soon," she said. "Thought I'd let you know so you could start lookin' for someone else."

Abby's father put down the newspaper. "What's the problem now, Coralee? I'm sure we can work things out."

"No problem, this time. Just more money."

"You want a raise?" There was surprise in Abby's father's voice. "But you're making more than the going rate. We've been paying you extra because you keep an eye on Bobby whenever Abby and Mrs. Baynes are out of town!"

Abby's nose wrinkled at the slightly scorched smell of the toast. She swung down the arms of the toaster and pulled out the bread before it burned around the edges. She carried the plate of toast and a glass of milk to the table and sat next to her father. His forehead was wrinkled with concern.

"I honestly don't see how we can give you another raise, Coralee," he said.

"I ain't askin' for a raise," she said. "I told you I was fixin' to leave."

"But you said something about more money."

Coralee leaned back and put her hands on her hips. "It's not *you* payin' me more money," she announced. "It's those defense plants. My girlfriend said I'd be crazy not to go talk to Lockheed. They're hirin' women as well as men to build their warplanes, and they're payin' good money, lots more than I can get keepin' house—yours or anybody else's."

"Can you please give us a couple of weeks, a little time to find someone to take your place?"

"Sure," Coralee said. "I'll try to stay on till you get somebody. I'm just thinkin' you may not find anybody. Them defense plants are movin' into Los Angeles fast as they can make 'em. They're puttin' out big ads in both the papers, too." She looked a little smug. "Aside from the money, my girlfriend says it's our patriotic duty to work there."

"All sorts of jobs are important," Abby's father explained. "All the jobs that had to be done before still must be taken care of, and—"

Coralee interrupted. "You know what I mean, Mr. Baynes. You got two jobs. You work all day at your bank job, and you been doing that civil defense stuff, too. Comin' home late most nights. I don't want two jobs. One's plenty for me."

"We all have to help. Mrs. Baynes signed up to do some volunteer work at the Red Cross."

"When she remembers." Coralee gave a sniff. "Anyhow, I'm goin' to be off to do defense work soon. The world is sure changin'.'"

Abby's father sighed and picked up his paper again. "You're right, Coralee. The world is changing."

"All sorts of things is gonna be different," Coralee said knowingly. She pointed at the butter that Abby was spreading on her bread. "My girlfriend said that butter's gonna go for sure. Military men are gonna eat it all. And once the gov'ment starts rationin', there's a lot of things, like meat and such, we ain't never gonna see till this war's over."

"I'm sure that we'll have to do without a few things, but I don't think it will be that bad," Abby's father said.

"I'm just tellin' you what my girlfriend told me."

"I think your girlfriend might have received some faulty information."

With an injured sigh, Coralee turned and marched back into the kitchen, tugging the door shut behind her. It closed with a squeak. Abby turned to her father. "I think it's true about the butter. I heard that on the radio, too."

Bobby looked up from his comic book, his expression hopeful. "Did they say anything about turnips?" he asked.

Abby looked at Bobby in surprise. "You mean you haven't heard about that, either?" she asked seriously. "That's all we'll have left to eat—turnips. Oh, yes, and spinach. Things our servicemen refuse to eat."

For a moment Bobby looked horrified, then he scowled at Abby as he realized that she'd been teasing.

Dad laughed, then looked at his wristwatch. "Time for me to get to work," he said, pushing back his chair and standing up.

"Aren't you going to tell Mom what Coralee said?" Bobby asked.

He shook his head. "Your mother needs her sleep," he answered. "Coralee will be sure to tell her when she comes down to breakfast."

At the mention of her mother, Abby wanted to get away, to leave the house in a hurry. She jumped to her feet and said, "Come on, Bobby. Give me a minute to put on my lipstick, and I'll walk with you to school."

March was one of Abby's favorite months. It was a mixed-up month, with days of blustery rain and cold scattered among days of sun and the crisp, fresh air of spring. As she and Bobby walked down Harvard Avenue toward Hollywood Boulevard, Abby kicked at a few of the large curled and drying magnolia leaves that still littered the sidewalk.

"Does the war scare you?" Bobby asked. Without waiting for an answer, he said, "It scares me. Stan, one of the guys at school, has an uncle who's an Army officer, and he said that the Japanese Army is going to try to land on the California coast. He said they'll land in the dead of night somewhere around Santa Monica."

"The Japanese aren't going to tell Stan's uncle their plans," Abby said. "Think about it. If you were a general and wanted to capture a country, you'd keep your plans secret, wouldn't you?"

"Yeah, I guess," Bobby said, but he didn't sound convinced. "Stan said our Army's taking over the Walt Disney studio in Burbank!"

Abby was puzzled. "Why are they doing that?"

"So they can protect Lockheed. It's right next to Disney's studio. The Japs are going to try to bomb Lockheed and Douglas and Vultee—all the defense plants." He tucked his books under one arm. Pointing up at the sky as though he were aiming a gun, he yelled, "Ack-ack-ack-ack" until Abby begged him to stop.

They had reached Hollywood Boulevard. "So long," Bobby said. He stepped into the street, poised to run across at the first break in traffic.

"Watch that car," Abby called. "Be careful."

Bobby looked back over his shoulder. "You're not my mother!" he shouted with a grin.

He dashed quickly across the street and down half a block to the entrance of the Hollywood Professional School, where a few kids had gathered. A boy a little taller than Bobby left the group and walked over to meet him. Abby recognized him. Stanley Abbot. She didn't like him. There was something sneaky about him. She wished that Bobby would make other friends. Bobby, however, seemed fascinated by Stanley. Abby sighed.

Mama had enrolled Bobby in Hollywood Professional because its classwork was arranged to fit the in-school, out-of-school schedules of its students, most of whom worked in films or radio. It meant that Bobby could leave class for auditions, Mama said. To Abby's surprise, Dad had fought against it. He wanted Bobby to go to the local public school instead. But Mama had persisted until he had given in.

"Bobby deserves a chance at stardom, too," Mama had said. "Look at that beautiful face!" Her voice had softened, and she'd looked at Bobby with so much love that Abby had been amazed. "He takes after my side of the family," she had added proudly.

Dad had begun talking in a low voice.

Abby could tell that he was choosing his words carefully. He didn't want to come right out and tell Mama that no matter how handsome Bobby was, he didn't have the talent to make it. "You're spending so much time with Abby's career," Dad had said, "how will you find time to take Bobby to auditions, too?"

"Abby's career?" Mama had sneaked a sideways glance in Abby's direction. "Things are a little slow for her now. In the meantime . . ." She gave Bobby another fond look and firmly added, "They *both* deserve a chance."

Now and then Bobby was called for an audition. He rarely got a job, however, unless all a director wanted was an extra with an angelic face. Poor Bobby had no talent as an actor, and neither his mother's encouragement nor drama lessons were any help. Fortunately, Bobby himself didn't seem to care. But Mama did.

A large, red Hollywood streetcar rumbled to a stop in the center of the street. Abby—her nickel fare ready in her hand—ran out to the safety island and jumped on board.

At lunch Abby and her best friend, Mary Lou Robertson, settled on the lawn in front of Hollywood High School's Fine Arts Building and opened their lunch bags.

"Tell me about the premiere," Mary Lou said.

Abby made a face. "The movie was terrible."

"I don't care about the movie. What about the stars who were there?"

"Ah, the stars," Abby said. She laid her lunch sack on the lawn, looked down her nose and stared haughtily. "Dahling," she said firmly, "surely you realize that all these fans are here to adore beautiful, gorgeous *me!*"

Then she slumped, stuck her hands into imaginary pockets, lowered her voice and stammered, "Well . . . uh . . . uh . . . now, Joan . . . uh . . . Crawford . . . it's possible that uh . . . uh . . . some of them came to see me. I mean ever since my movie . . . uh . . . *Mr. Smith Goes to Washington*, won an . . uh . . . uh . . . Academy Award, I've been kinda popular . . . uh . . . myself."

Mary Lou laughed. "You do Jimmy Stewart perfectly! And you're so funny, Abby. But really, tell me about the premiere!"

Abby sighed. "It was awful. Linda Larkin was there, looking gorgeous, of course. She pointed out that she was working and I wasn't. She—she even made fun of the way I was dressed." She paused. "But that wasn't the worst part." She told Mary Lou about the horrible fish-faced woman who had reappeared in her dream that night.

Mary Lou was the first person Abby had ever been able to confide in. The two of them shared secrets they couldn't whisper to anyone else. Even so, Abby's cheeks flushed with embarrassment as she spoke.

"I shouldn't have brought it up," she mumbled, dumping the contents of her lunch sack onto her lap.

Mary Lou, whose pompadour had come loose, paused to anchor the swirl of dark blond hair with a bobby pin. "I don't blame you for being unhappy, especially about what you were wearing."

Abby found herself trying to defend her mother. "Oh, the dress doesn't matter that much. It means a lot to Mama—the days when I was so young and cute."

"But you're not a cute little toddler now." Mary Lou's blue eyes sparked. "Your mother makes you wear that outfit. She makes you try to look years younger than you are."

"The woman and what she said to me bothers me more than the dress," Abby insisted.

"But think about it, Abby," Mary Lou went on. "The woman asked if you used to be Cookie Baynes, and you said to yourself, 'I *am* Cookie Baynes.' Don't you see? That's the problem. You're not Cookie Baynes any longer, no matter what your mother tries to make you believe. You're *Abby* Baynes."

Abby was shaken. "Mary Lou, I don't want to give

all that up, either. I remember what it was like to have people tell me that I could make them laugh or cry. I loved acting in front of the cameras. I loved the excitement, and I loved the make-believe. It was the happiest part of my life."

Mary Lou leaned forward and put a hand on Abby's arm. "You don't have to give it up," she said. "You're just as talented as you ever were—probably more so."

"Then why don't directors call anymore? What happened to all those parts that were perfect for Cookie Baynes?"

"Weren't you listening to what I said? You're not a little girl any longer. You can make a new career by being yourself, by being *Abby* Baynes."

Abby smiled wryly. "Do you really think that Judy Garland and Jane Powell and Linda Larkin will move over and make room for me?"

"Why not?" Mary Lou made a face. "What has Linda Larkin got that you haven't got, besides Max Factor pancake makeup an inch thick!"

"A super figure," Abby said.

"Maybe she wears falsies," Mary Lou said.

"Falsies?" Abby said in a syrupy voice. "The rest of us have A-cups and B-cups. But Linda's given new meaning to bra size. Hers are teacups—real ones."

They burst out laughing.

"Mean, but funny," Mary Lou chuckled.

Abby thought a moment, then said, "I've known Linda since we were toddlers. I've never liked her, and I've never liked her mother. Linda had a couple of lines in one of my pictures—*Angel Babies*—and whenever she was on the set her mother kept glaring at me with so much hatred it scared me." Abby took a bite of her sandwich, then added, "The last day of filming I was walking past the woman and she reached out and pinched me!"

"Stage mothers are monsters!" Mary Lou declared, then added apologetically, "Most of them, that is."

Abby shrugged. "*All* of them, Mary Lou. I know. Mama lorded it over Mrs. Larkin then, and now she has a fit any time she reads about any movie Linda is in."

Mary Lou took a little bite of her tuna sandwich. "Forget Linda Larkin and think about what I said. I know you've got talent. Those routines you do—they make me laugh every time."

"I learned some of those routines from Rusty Drew. Remember him? He was one of the best song-and-dance men I ever saw, and the best comic I'll ever work with."

"Who could ever forget? Ta da, ta da da," Mary Lou sang, mimicking a song that had become famous in an early Cookie Baynes movie.

"He taught me so much about comedy—how to do a slow double take, take a one-second beat before coming out with the punch line of a joke, the wide-eyed stare. Rusty was wonderful. I missed him so much when he died."

"Well, if you want to keep Rusty's memory alive, you should be putting what he taught you to good use," Mary Lou said. "Frankly, I think if you're not getting parts, it's not your fault, it's your agent's."

Abby swallowed the last bite of her sandwich with a gulp. "Mama says that Al Jerome is the best actor's agent in this town. She thinks we're lucky to have him."

"Sometimes you make me so mad, Abby." Mary Lou blew up her empty paper bag like a balloon and smashed it with a bang. "I don't know too much about the movie industry, but I do know that your agent is supposed to get you auditions. All yours does is send you to entertain at Eastern Star Luncheons."

"Those luncheon jobs keep my name and face before the public." With a shock Abby realized she was parroting her mother's words, and she felt her face flush with embarrassment.

"I remember the year we met, when we were both in the ninth grade and new at Le Conte Junior High School," Mary Lou said. "You told me all about a big studio party you'd gone to. You mentioned some agent at the party who asked a lot of questions about your career. He seemed interested. Remember?"

Abby nodded her head slowly. "Yes. I remember. He was Simon Harkins. He's head of Major Artists."

"There! You see! That's one of the biggest talent agencies in Hollywood." Mary Lou smiled and held out her hands, palms up. "Why don't you talk to him, Abby? Find out what he has to say about a career for you."

"Maybe I should," Abby said, but all she could think of was Mama, and how livid with anger she'd be if she ever found out Abby had gone behind Al's back.

"I just wish I were an agent," Mary Lou said. "I'd get you lots of parts, because I believe in you."

Abby's appreciative grin froze as Mary Lou continued. "You'd be famous again, which would make your mother happy—"

"No!" Abby blurted. "Sure, Mama would be happy, but I don't want a career just for her. I want it—I *need* it for myself. Don't you understand?"

Mary Lou shook her head, her eyes puzzled. "I can understand that you want a career, but how can you *need* to be an actress?"

"I mean that a career in acting is something I can't live without."

For a moment Mary Lou studied Abby. Then she said, "You've already had more fame and excitement than most of the people of the world have ever dreamed of having. Isn't that enough?"

"No," Abby answered. "What matters is how I feel inside myself, knowing that I'm a good actress, that if I'm just given the chance . . ." She stopped and leaned forward intently. "Let me explain this way. I want to be an actress the way all the other girls we know want to meet the men of their dreams and get married someday."

"Hi." The deep voice next to her ear startled Abby so much that she jumped.

"Luke! It's you!"

With an easy familiarity Luke settled next to Abby, resting his strong arm around her shoulders. Luke rarely talked about her career, and Abby was glad. Once he'd told her, "Oh, sure, I guess it's impressive that you were once a star, but I don't care one way or the other what you were like in the past." He'd kissed the tip of her nose and added, "All I care about is Abby now."

"So . . . tell me. What were you talking about?" Luke asked. He grinned at Mary Lou. "It must have been pretty deep stuff. There's still a wrinkle on Mary Lou's forehead."

"Just girl talk," Mary Lou said, smiling in return. "Nothing we're going to tell you."

Luke seemed to have something on his mind, anyway. "I've heard some rumors about a new school policy," he said.

"What are they going to do to us next?" Mary Lou asked with a groan. "Is this Mr. Foley's idea or Mr. Winchester's?"

"It's not just for Hollywood High," Luke said. "It's going to be an all-school policy." He sounded so serious that Abby was startled. "It's for all the guys who are seniors and want to enlist in one of the armed forces. If their grades have been okay for the first semester of their senior year, they'll be automatically graduated and given diplomas. That means they'll be free to join up."

Abby's eyes widened. "If they're eighteen, you mean."

"Sooner, if they can get their parents to sign for them."

Abby clutched his arm. "Luke, why are you telling us this?"

"Abby," he said, "I'm trying to say that I'm sure I can talk my folks into signing for me." His words seemed to come from the other end of a long, icy tunnel. "I'm going to enlist in the Navy."

"Luke! No!" Abby gasped and reached for his hand, holding it tightly. "I don't want you to go."

"I have to go," Luke said. "You should be proud of me, Abby."

"I—I am," she stammered, wishing she really felt that way. Patriotic? Yes, but not when it came to Luke. "I—I'm scared. The news we get . . . and the awful war scenes in the newsreels—people screaming and running, and bombs dropping." She shuddered. "Luke, can't you at least wait three months until you're eighteen?"

"Then I'd get drafted into the Army. I'd rather be in the Navy. If I enlist before my eighteenth birthday, I'll get a choice."

The bell rang. Mary Lou got to her feet and dusted off her skirt. Luke folded his long legs and stood up, reaching down a hand to help Abby to her feet.

"I'll come over tonight, and we'll talk some more about it," Luke whispered. "Around eight o'clock okay? It's Friday, no school tomorrow, so your mother won't mind, will she?"

"Eight o'clock's fine," Abby answered. Still holding Luke's hand, she walked with him and Mary Lou toward the science building, where they shared a chemistry class.

Abby wished there were somewhere else to meet him. Each time Abby went out with Luke her mother made some disparaging remark about him. Mama wouldn't be happy about his visit, and she'd probably let him know.

"He's just a working-class guy," Mama would tell Abby. "Why don't you go out with some of those nice boys you met at the studio? What about that Johnny Erwin who's under contract to Fox?"

"Johnny Erwin's not interested in me."

"Johnny's got a real future in films. I know talent. I can tell."

Mama just couldn't understand that Luke was special and kind and wonderful to be with, and it wouldn't have mattered to Abby if he were a streetcar conductor. But now, perhaps, Mama would never get the chance to understand, not if Luke were leaving Abby to fight in a war thousands of miles away. Suddenly the pain of loneliness, unlike anything she'd ever before experienced, gripped her. Abby stumbled as the thought hit her: *I think I may be in love with him!*

3

$\mathcal{A}$s soon as her last class was over, Abby walked up Highland to Hollywood Boulevard and waited for a streetcar. Since it was Friday, the sidewalks were already crowded with servicemen on weekend leave, drawn to the excitement of Hollywood. They peered hopefully into the faces of people passing by, waiting to see a movie star.

A cluster of marines stood on the corner across the

street from Abby, watching a film crew at work in front of the Hollywood Hotel. A young woman in a blue dress strolled down the walk from the main entrance, then repeated the action over and over again. People who watched a film being shot always expected to see a story taking place. They couldn't believe how often every scene was repeated. They couldn't believe how boring it was to make a movie. Abby sighed. *Boring, yes, but wonderful,* she thought.

Next door to the hotel, men in uniform swarmed around the footprints and handprints of the stars that had been captured in cement in front of Grauman's Chinese Theatre.

With a clanging of its bell, the streetcar at last pulled up to the corner, and Abby climbed on board. Twenty minutes later they had reached Harvard Avenue.

As Abby jumped from the bottom step of the streetcar, she saw Bobby and Stanley standing on the sidewalk a few feet away. Their heads were close together. They were both so intent on something Stanley was holding that they were oblivious to everything around them. Feeling mischievous, Abby crept up behind them.

Poised to shout "Boo!" she stopped and stared openmouthed as she saw what Stanley was doing.

In his hand was a little booklet, not much bigger than a matchbook. It contained photos of a nude woman in an obscene pose. As Stanley fanned the booklet, the woman looked as though she were moving.

Abby's right hand shot out and grabbed Stanley's wrist. Dropping her books, she shoved Bobby aside and snatched the booklet from Stanley's hand. "Give that to me!" she shouted.

Stanley wiggled and tugged his arm from her grasp. "It's mine!" he cried in a determined voice. Bobby edged away, his eyes wide with guilt and fear.

"Not anymore it isn't!" Abby snapped. She tore the booklet into little pieces, throwing the scraps of paper on the ground.

"That wasn't yours! Y-you ruined it!" he yelled.

"Where did you get it?" She took a step toward him.

"None of your business." His fury slid into a smirk. "What are you so mad about? Seeing nudie pictures isn't going to hurt your precious baby brother."

Abby motioned toward the school. "You could be suspended if your principal found out about it."

"About what?" Stanley grinned and gestured toward the scraps of paper blowing down the sidewalk. "You tore it up. No evidence."

Frustrated, Abby picked up her books, turned to Bobby and ordered, "Let's go home."

Silently Bobby crossed the boulevard with her and headed up the hill toward Franklin Avenue.

"You didn't need to get so mad at Stanley," Bobby finally said. "It wasn't so bad."

"It *was* bad. Women—well, women shouldn't be thought of like that. Promise me, Bobby. If Stanley gets any more of those things, you won't look at them. All right?"

For just an instant Bobby hesitated; then a flicker crossed his eyes. "All right," he said smoothly, "if *you'll* promise not to embarrass me in front of my friends again."

"I didn't mean to embarrass you."

"Well, you did."

"I reacted to what I saw. I guess I didn't take time to think." She sighed. "I'd probably do the same thing again."

"Then I won't promise."

"All right," Abby said. "Then I promise. That's fair." The last car passed and the street was temporarily clear of traffic. "Come on!" She ran across the street, Bobby beating her to the other side, and started up the hill into Laughlin Park.

As Abby and Bobby walked into the house, the telephone rang. "I'll get it," Abby called.

The voice on the other end of the line surprised her. It was their elderly neighbor from up the hill, Mrs. Fitch.

Mama didn't like Mrs. Fitch. "The woman's absurd, with that thin, orange hair and pink hair bow," she'd said.

And Mrs. Rice, the gossip of Laughlin Park, had once told Abby, "She has a *past*. I heard from a reliable source that Madeleine Fitch was a showgirl with a *reputation* until she feathered her nest by marrying a wealthy stage-door Johnny."

Abby didn't wonder or care about Mrs. Fitch's past. She liked her neighbor, who had fascinating stories to tell about weeklong parties in palaces in Europe. Mrs. Fitch lived alone, with only a houseboy to take care of her. Sometimes her loneliness was even more obvious than her bright hair and hair bows.

"Abby?" Mrs. Fitch said. "I'm glad you answered the phone and not your mother. She'd never believe what I'm going to tell you." She lowered her voice. Abby could almost picture her looking from side to side as she whispered, "I'm afraid there are spies in Laughlin Park."

Abby closed her eyes for a moment and took a deep breath. Mrs. Fitch had always been bright and alert, with a vital energy that seemed to glow through her light blue eyes. This apprehension was unlike her. "What makes you think that?" Abby asked slowly.

"Don't humor me, Abby," Mrs. Fitch said. "I'm not dotty. Listen! For the past two nights I've seen lights flashing on and off in the house of the couple who live on the side of the hill. I was finally able to find out their name, and it's German!"

Abby tried to ask the right question. "Do you mean you've seen a signal light? Like on a battleship?"

"Nothing that obvious. I've studied their house with binoculars during the daytime, and can't see a thing that would look like a signal light. But they're sending some sort of signals. I know it!"

"Who would they signal to?"

"I don't know. Japanese spies? It's no secret the Japanese are planning to invade the California coast."

Abby shivered. Everyone who lived in Los Angeles was afraid of that possibility.

"Maybe you should tell some official about the lights," Abby said.

Mrs. Fitch's voice suddenly sounded older and tired. "I did call Cecil B. DeMille, since he's our block warden.

He became very gentlemanly and patient. He said he'd look into it, but I know he didn't believe me. That's where you come in, Abby. You can see the house I'm talking about from your yard. It's the dark brick on the side of the hill, facing DeMille Drive, two houses in from Linwood. Will you please take a look tonight, Abby, and tell me if you see those flashing lights?"

She's really frightened, Abby thought. "Of course I will," she replied. "And I'll call you tomorrow and give you a report."

Mrs. Fitch sighed with relief. "Thank you, Abby. You're a good girl, even if you don't come to see me very often." Abby had to smile. Mrs. Fitch certainly wasn't subtle. "I know," Mrs. Fitch went on. "Instead of using the telephone, why don't you come over to visit and tell me what you saw? I'll have Jiro make some lemon sponge tea cakes. He's a very good cook, you know."

She hung up without waiting for an answer. Abby didn't really believe there were German spies in Laughlin Park signaling to the Japanese, but it wouldn't hurt to make Mrs. Fitch happy.

The phone rang again, and this time it was Mary Lou. "I forgot to let you know when I saw you at school," she bubbled. "I signed both of us up to work in the Red Cross Hut tomorrow morning. They need volunteers to cut cartoons out of copies of *The Saturday Evening Post* and *Collier's* and paste them in scrapbooks for the war effort."

"What do cartoon scrapbooks have to do with the war effort?"

"They're for the servicemen who get wounded. It's something to cheer them up while they're in the hospital."

"Oh." Abby shivered, thinking of Luke.

"Can you come?" Mary Lou asked. "Ten o'clock?"

"Sure," Abby said. "I'll be there."

"Did I tell you I'm going out with Dennis tonight?"

"You mean the kid who's in eleventh grade?"

Mary Lou sighed. "Well, at least he's tall. If what Luke says is true, by the time we graduate, there may not be any boys left in the senior class."

Abby didn't want to think about what Luke had told them. "I've got to go," she told Mary Lou. "I'll see you tomorrow. Ten o'clock."

As Abby put down the phone, Coralee appeared in the doorway. "You want an early dinner?"

Abby was startled. "Shouldn't you ask my mother that?"

"Your ma's goin' out," Coralee said. "She told me there was no sense stayin' in when the mister won't get home till late. So it's just you and Bobby and me here for dinner."

Good! Abby stood up. If Mama weren't there when Luke came, he wouldn't get the frosty looks and snobbish remarks. "Just make dinner whenever it's easy for you, Coralee. Bobby and I won't care."

She heard the radio in her mother's bedroom. A band was playing "Our Love Affair" and Mama was singing along with it. Usually the song, which was from the Judy Garland–Mickey Rooney movie *Strike Up the Band*, reminded Mama that Linda Larkin had won a good-sized speaking part in that movie and that Abby hadn't even been called for the audition. But that evening, for some reason, her mother's mood seemed to be good anyway.

Abby waited outside the door until the song had finished and another band had started playing the sentimental "There I Go," then knocked.

"Come in, come in!" Mama called cheerfully.

Abby entered the large room with its matching bedspread and long, flowing curtains of peach satin. Mama was reclining on a cream-colored chaise longue, propped up by small, lacy pillows, painting her nails.

"Passion pink," Mama said, holding up a hand. "Isn't it a wonderful color? And I bought a lipstick to match."

Abby sat on the edge of the nearest twin bed. "Can we talk about Bobby?" she asked.

"Is it terribly important? I'm going out to dinner, and it takes a while to get dressed." Mama waved the fingers of her right hand in the air, then blew on her nails.

"It won't take long," Abby said. Before her mother could interrupt, she recounted what had happened with Stanley.

Mama frowned. "It really wasn't Bobby's fault," she said. "How would he know what Stanley was going to show him?"

"It's Stanley I'm worried about," Abby said. "He's a bad kid, Mama. Mean, too. I think Bobby should make other friends."

Mama carefully put another coat of polish on her left thumbnail before she answered. "Stanley's father is a very important director at Universal," she said. "Stanley's a good contact for Bobby. He might even be for you."

"Mama!" Abby cried. "That shouldn't matter!"

For the first time Mama gave Abby her full attention. "Well, it does matter," she said. "In this town everything matters. Besides, Stanley's a smart kid. He gets top grades. Maybe he'll be a good influence on Bobby in that direction." Her forehead wrinkled with concern. "I hope you didn't upset him too much."

Abby was shocked. "But those obscene pictures—"

Mama interrupted. "If it will make you happy, I'll have Frank talk to Bobby. Now, do me a favor, darling. Get my new blue crepe dress out of the closet and see if it needs pressing."

"That's all you're going to say about it?"

"That's all that needs to be said. Don't scowl like that. You'll wrinkle early." Mama sighed elaborately. "Please, let's not argue when I'm in such a good mood!"

Abby reluctantly opened the door to Mama's closet and found the blue dress. She held it up, turning it around on the hanger. "It looks fine to me," she said.

"Then run off, Sweetie, and let me get dressed." Mama began to hum under her breath with the music.

"You and Mrs. Rice must be going to some very nice place."

Mama glanced up sharply, then shrugged and relaxed again. "We haven't decided. Maybe Chasen's, maybe Perino's or maybe Musso and Frank." She turned up the volume on the radio and swung her legs from the chaise. "Go on now. Scoot."

The band was playing "I've Got My Love to Keep Me Warm," and Mama began to sing along. Abby closed the bedroom door behind her and leaned against it. She should have gone to Dad in the first place. Usually Dad stayed in the background and allowed Mama to run the show, but Abby could count on him when she needed to. Maybe she had overreacted with Bobby and Stanley. If Dad agreed, she'd believe him, whereas with Mama . . . Abby shook her head in disbelief as she recalled Mama's words: "Stanley's a good contact."

By the time Luke arrived that evening, Mama, her cheeks pink with excitement, had left in a cloud of Chanel. Coralee had gone to her room next to the kitchen to listen to her favorite program, *One Man's Family*, on her bedside radio. Bobby was in the breakfast room, talking to Stanley on the telephone.

"Both my parents are out," Abby said as she led Luke into the living room. "They won't be back until close to ten, so we can talk without being interrupted. We can even play records."

Luke grinned. "Good. I was going to take you driving somewhere to get you alone, but now we can stay here. Let's put on some records and dance."

"Dance? I thought you wanted to talk about—about enlisting?"

"There isn't much to say about it."

"Yes there is, because I want to try to talk you out of it."

Luke took both her hands. "Not now, Abby. Dance with me. And while we're dancing, don't go over and over in your mind any arguments you want to use with me. Just think of *me*. Promise?"

He looked at her so earnestly, she had to agree. "All right. I promise," she said. "I've got a new Benny Goodman record and that Duke Ellington jazz thing you like so much."

"I'll pick the records," Luke told her with a grin. "And I warn you, they're all going to be slow. No swing, no jitterbug, not even a balboa."

Luke went through some of Abby's records, choosing carefully and stacking them above the turntable. "We'll start with 'Always,' " he said.

He turned on the record player and held out his arms as the record dropped into place. Abby moved into them, resting her cheek against his chin and wrapping her left arm around his shoulders. He held her right hand snugly against his chest, and pulled her even closer. The music was dreamy, the words a little sad. *How could they count on an "always" if Luke went away to fight?*

Abby tried to concentrate on Luke—the slightly salty smell of his skin and his warm breath against her ear. She closed her eyes as they drifted, barely moving, to the slow beat. The music ended, and the phonograph made a series of loud clicks as its arm came back to drop another record on the turntable. Luke and Abby didn't move. When the music began again they automatically flowed into its rhythm.

Luke's lips brushed her forehead, and Abby smiled, raising her chin.

"I'm going upstairs now." The voice behind her startled Abby. She jumped away from Luke and stared. Bobby grinned at her. "You guys are boring," he said. "I'm going to listen to *I Love a Mystery*." He tilted his head and studied Luke. "What's it worth to you if I don't come downstairs again?"

"Get out of here, Bobby!" Abby tried to sound stern, but she couldn't help laughing.

"I'm going, I'm going. And I won't bother you again. Good night, Luke."

"Good to see you, Bobby," Luke said as Bobby clattered up the stairs.

"We don't need so much light in here," Luke said. He turned off all the lights but one small, dim table lamp in a corner. "Much better," he said and enfolded Abby even more snugly than before.

The next record dropped, and Luke lifted Abby's chin to kiss her. As though it were part of the music and the dance, she eagerly kissed him back. The music flowed around them as they stood, lightly swaying, their lips touching, their bodies pressed together. Luke's kisses were not the light, sometimes fumbling kisses Abby had known in the past. They were so intense Abby began to tremble. She was part of the music, part of Luke, unable to think, only able to respond.

Luke's lips moved to Abby's neck, then down to the hollow at the base of her throat. She shivered, dizzy and drowning in her own rapid heartbeat.

"Abby, I love you," Luke whispered in her ear. "You don't know how much I love you. Please tell me that you love me. Tell me."

Luke loved her. Somebody loved her! Abby pressed even closer and murmured, "Yes, I love you! I do love you!"

"Oh, Abby, Abby!" His kiss was so overpowering that Abby could hardly breathe. Frightened, she pushed him away.

They staggered to the nearby sofa and fell against the cushions. He bent to kiss her again. "Luke," Abby whispered, "we have to stop."

"No," he said. "We love each other. Whatever we do is all right." His fingers crept under the back of her sweater and fumbled with the hooks that fastened her bra.

With all her strength, Abby shoved against his chest. "You've got to stop, Luke. I've never felt like this. It scares me."

Luke raised his head and looked into her eyes. "Abby, don't you understand? I'll be going away to fight soon. I might never come back."

"Don't say that!" She shuddered.

"You say you love me. If you really loved me you'd want to prove it, wouldn't you?"

Terrified by emotions she didn't understand, Abby cried, "If you really loved me you wouldn't ask!"

Abby could see the hurt and sorrow in Luke's eyes. "Oh, Abby," he said, "please don't look at me like that. Don't be afraid of me. I'd never hurt you. Never!"

He pulled her up to a sitting position and tenderly stroked back her hair from her face.

"My parents gave their permission for me to enlist," he said in a low voice. "They're going to sign for me. I'm glad about that, but I don't know what's going to happen to me, Abby. I want to serve my country, but I don't know what it will be like to kill someone. I don't really want to know." He shuddered. "I guess maybe I'm scared. I thought if anyone would understand, you would."

"Oh, Luke," Abby whispered. As he pulled her closer she rested her head against his chest, aching for him. She wished she could assure him that he'd be safe. But she couldn't. The memory of the newsreel scenes of bombings, people running, and bodies lying on the ground was too vivid. People had died. People would continue to die in the war.

But not Luke. No! It couldn't happen to Luke.

He continued to caress her hair, her face, and her neck. His fingertips made her skin tingle.

"All I'll have of you will be a memory," he murmured. "I guess I'm selfish, but I'd hoped you'd care about me enough to want to give me a very special memory. It would be a special memory for you, too, Abby. It would bind us together."

Abby groaned. "I can't. Please, Luke, don't make it so hard on me."

"Think about it. I'm going away, maybe forever."

He kissed her again, but Abby twisted away. "Luke, you know how I feel about you," she said in a shaky voice. "You're not being fair."

He stood and faced her. "How about you? Are you being fair? You let me fall in love with you, then you turn me down."

Her face burned. For a moment she pressed her fingertips against her cheeks, unsuccessfully trying to cool them. She couldn't keep the tears from her eyes. "Stop, Luke, you're confusing me. You've never talked to me like this before. I thought you knew what kind of girl I was."

"Abby, honey, is that what's bothering you?" Luke's voice became tender, and he took a step toward her. "It's not 'good girl' or 'bad girl' anymore. The world's different now. The war's made it different." Luke held out his arms. "Don't be mad at me, Abby," he began. "Let me hold you. Let me help you understand."

"The war's made it different." Without making any confessions, that was just what some of the girls at school had been murmuring in the hallways.

Is it true? Abby asked herself. *Am I out of step with more than just my stage act?*

No.

Her love for Luke was the best part of her life, and she couldn't let it go all wrong, but she wasn't going to weaken. Luke had to leave. Right away.

Abby ran through the entrance hall and to the front door, flinging it open.

"I don't want to talk about it," she said. "I don't want to talk to you at all right now. Go away, Luke. Please!"

"Abby," Luke pleaded and took a step toward her.

———

47

Mutely, she shook her head.

"Okay," Luke whispered. He walked through the door and down the porch steps.

Abby heard his car start as she slowly closed the door and bolted it. She leaned against the door, resting her head on her arms. A miserable ache spread through her entire body. What had Luke done? What had *she* done?

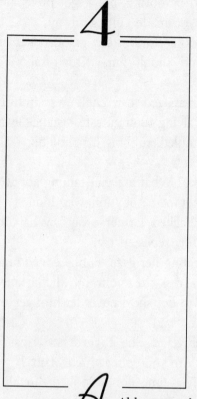

4

As Abby waited for her racing heart to slow down and the trembling of her body to subside, she heard a soft chuckle come from the direction of the stairway.

She whirled, gasping, as Bobby stepped forward from the shadows on the first landing and walked down the short flight of stairs to join her.

"That was better than a movie," he snickered.

Abby was mortified. "You were spying on us!"

He nodded. "That's right. I thought you'd just dance, and it would be boring, but it got pretty interesting. I'm kinda sorry you made Luke go away."

Abby was so furious she grabbed her brother by the shoulders and shook him. "Don't talk like that!" she yelled.

Bobby managed to wrench away from her grasp. He ran into the living room, a safe distance away. "You hurt me," he grumbled, rubbing his shoulder. "That's going to cost you more."

"Cost me? What are you talking about?" Fighting to control her temper, Abby followed him.

Bobby backed farther away. "What do you mean, cost me?" Abby repeated.

Not meeting her gaze, Bobby edged onto the far end of the sofa across the room. "If Mama knew what Luke wanted you to do, she'd never let him get anywhere near you again," he said.

Abby shivered. She hugged her arms, rubbing them vigorously. "Are you going to tell Mama?"

"No!" This time Bobby looked directly at her. "Not if you pay me. Then I won't tell."

"Blackmail?" It was difficult for Abby to believe what she was hearing.

"Yeah. I guess that's what it's called."

"Who gave you that idea, Bobby?"

Guilt swept across his face. "I—I thought it up myself."

"You were talking on the phone with Stanley, weren't you?"

"What if I was?"

"Stanley told you what to do, didn't he?"

Bobby's lower lip curled out in a pout. "It doesn't make any difference who thought up the idea. You're going to have to pay me—uh—five dollars. No, make that ten dollars. Wait—twenty! Yeah, twenty dollars or I'll tell."

Abby closed her eyes and took a long, slow breath.

"Well?" Bobby asked, his voice uncertain.

Abby leaned forward, looking directly into Bobby's eyes. "Go ahead," she said. "Tell."

Bobby's jaw hung open. Stammering, he managed to ask, "Y-you really w-want me to tell? Then Mama won't let Luke come back."

Abby just shrugged. "Maybe I don't want him to come back," she said, but her entire body cried for Luke.

Bobby slumped down, his head against the back cushions of the sofa.

"I'm disgusted with you," Abby said. "That was a horrible, mean thing to do."

He sniffled and wiped his nose on his sleeve. "I didn't want to be mean," he whimpered. "I just needed some money. Stanley said that would be a good way to get some, and I thought it would be funny to spy on you. I didn't think about making you mad or I wouldn't have done it. I'm sorry."

Abby's anger quickly turned to pity. She walked to the sofa and sat next to Bobby, resting an arm around his shoulders. "Don't cry," she said.

But tears ran down his cheeks. "I never do anything right," he said. "I'm always left out."

"What do you mean by that?" Abby asked.

"The other kids are always doing things I can't do."

"Like what?"

"Like every day we all walk down to the Thrifty drugstore on Western. The other kids get ice cream bars, and candy and comic books. Stuff like that. But I don't get enough allowance to buy all that stuff, and I hate it when I'm left out. Stanley said I should just grab a candy bar and put it in my pocket, and the clerk would never know the difference."

Abby gasped. "Bobby! That's stealing! You can't do that!"

His lower lip curled out. "You don't know what it's like. When you were my age, you had people all around you to give you whatever you wanted. I've heard Mama talk enough about it."

Abby's heart fell. She'd had no idea anything had been troubling Bobby. How was she going to help him when she couldn't even solve her own problems?

She stood up, pulling Bobby to his feet, and put her arm around him. "Would it help for now, if I gave you a couple of dollars?" she asked.

"Sure," he said with a shrug. "For now."

"All right," she told him. "Come on upstairs. I'll get it."

As Abby took the bills from her purse and handed them to him, she said, "We need to get one thing straight. Don't ever try spying on me again, Bobby. Understand?"

Bobby seemed to be recovering quickly from his bout of dejection. He raised his face to hers, and his eyes were wide and innocent. "I won't, Abby. Not ever again. I said I was sorry, and I mean it."

"And you can't steal candy bars."

"I won't, as long as you help me out."

Abby sighed. "I'll share some of my allowance with you. That's the best I can do."

"Thanks, Abby," Bobby said. He smiled angelically.

Abby reached to hug him, but he squirmed away. "No sickening stuff!" he said. He ran to his own bedroom, slamming the door.

Abby turned off her own bedroom light and walked to the east window, opening it wide so she could see the spectrum of lights from downtown Hollywood Boulevard. They were reflected by the thin cloud cover, bathing the city in a yellow glow. Lights from streets and houses dotted the hill beyond Western Avenue. Hollywood was like a miniature village spread out for her enjoyment. The view calmed her, as it always did. She watched a light from a house on the hill wink out, then another one.

Lights! She'd almost forgotten her promise to Mrs. Fitch!

Abby walked to the end of the hallway and out onto the second-floor terrace, which stretched the length of the house. When she reached the east edge of the terrace, she leaned against the low stucco wall and glanced up at the house Mrs. Fitch had told her to watch.

The trees blocked her view. She walked a few feet to

the right and took another look. Now she could see more clearly. There were two lights, one upstairs, one down. The figure of a woman appeared in the upstairs window. She stood there for a moment, then pulled shut the heavy drapes, snuffing out the light.

Abby took a step back. As the branches waved in the night breeze, the downstairs light briefly flickered, then went out.

Abby sighed. If there were tree branches between Mrs. Fitch's house and the flickering lights, that would explain it. No spies. No signal lights. Just branches cutting off the light and allowing it to shine again. Abby smiled.

"Who left these doors open? Who's out there?" Mama was highlighted in the open doorway.

"It's just me," Abby said. She hurried to join her mother, locking the doors carefully. Mama's cheeks were pink, and her hair swung loosely around her face. "You look so pretty," Abby cried.

Mama giggled. "I feel pretty," she answered.

"You and Mrs. Rice must have had a wonderful time."

"Yes, we did," Mama replied quietly.

"Where did you go?"

"Go? Oh, Chasen's. It was very nice."

Mama pulled a couple of stray bobby pins out of her hair. "By the way," she said. "I wangled a party invitation for you. Donald Shaddoe's tenth birthday party. It's tomorrow evening at the Shaddoes' Hollywood Hills estate. Every kid who's important in films is going to be there."

"Mama!" Abby complained. "I don't even know Donald Shaddoe."

Her mother looked shocked. "His father's Kenneth Shaddoe. He's a big wheel at Paramount."

"That's not what I meant. Of course I know who his father is, but I've never met Donald. And he's only ten! My gosh, Mama! I'd be so out of place!"

Mama gave a long, dramatic sigh. Her eyes burned as they drilled into Abby's. "I hope you know how it cuts me to the quick when I plan something that will help you, and you resist me every step of the way."

"I'm sorry, Mama," Abby murmured. "I just thought—"

"You just thought?" Mama mimicked. "Well, don't think. Just listen to me. The party is a big one. Close to four hundred invitations went out. There'll be people there of all ages, not just ten-year-olds." She paused. "Linda Larkin will be there."

Abby sighed. "How did you get the invitation? Through Mrs. Larkin?"

"Of course not!" Mama snapped. "Al arranged it."

"Al Jerome?"

"What other Al would go to so much trouble for you?"

"Mama, listen to me," Abby said, desperate because she knew her mother wouldn't. "I wasn't invited with the rest of the guests, because the Shaddoes didn't want me. I'd be too embarrassed to go to a party where I'm practically a gate-crasher."

Mama gripped Abby's shoulders. "You're going to go to that party, young lady, and you're going to thank Al for his kindness, and I won't hear another word about it. Do you understand me?"

"Yes, Mama," Abby whispered.

Mama let go of Abby and her eyes grew soft and gentle.

"Oh, Sweetie, I didn't mean to get mad. I just—well, this party means so much to me. It will be like old times. Al has already hired a limousine. We'll go in style. Remember when we used to arrive at a party, Cookie? It was always in a limo—remember?" Mama's face lit with pleasure.

It came back to Abby then, as it often did: The fresh new-car smell of the limousine mingled with the heavy fragrance of the gardenia corsages Mama always wore, Dad's grin of pleasure, Mama's eyes shining with excitement.

Mama would snuggle against Dad on one side, Abby on the other. When they'd arrive at the party, people would cluster around them, glad to see them all, eager to talk to Cookie Baynes, to be seen with Cookie Baynes, or just to be near her for a little while. And all evening long, Mama would watch over her, adjusting her ribbons and bows when they needed it and basking in the glow of fame.

"It meant a great deal to you, didn't it?" Abby asked.

"Of course it did," Mama said. "Didn't you enjoy it, too?"

Abby took a deep breath and answered honestly. "Yes, Mama. I did."

Mama grinned and hugged Abby. "We're going to

strut our stuff at this party, Cookie. We'll show that Mrs. Larkin a thing or two."

Abby couldn't answer. She was grateful when her mother blew her a goodnight kiss and went to her own bedroom, shutting the door behind her.

Abby got ready for bed in the darkness, then knelt down by her open window again. Out there, to the south and to the west, too far away to see, were Paramount, Twentieth Century Fox, MGM, and RKO, their lots filled with beautiful two-dimensional make-believe sets for the city's endless costume party. Abby had spent her entire childhood as an honored guest at that party. Everyone had loved her—the adorable girl who sang, tap-danced, and displayed a deep dimple on either side of her sweet smile. Then she grew up, and they didn't love her anymore. It was as if her invitation had been sent back, stamped, "Canceled." Abby hadn't realized how much she'd miss the party until she'd been left out.

With a rush of humiliation Abby's thoughts returned to the begged invitation to the Shaddoes' party. Abby buried her face in her hands. Who did Mama think she'd be kidding?

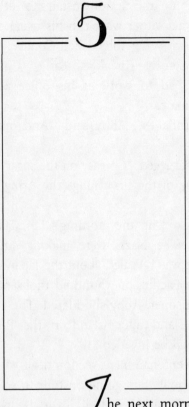

5

The next morning, just before nine, Abby telephoned Mrs. Fitch. Jiro answered. Mrs. Fitch was still asleep, and he didn't want to wake her.

"Please don't," Abby said. "Mrs. Fitch asked me to check something for her, so I did. Please tell her that I didn't see anything, and I'll come visit her tomorrow."

"She say you come today," he answered.

"I know I told her I would," Abby said, "but something has come up. Tell her I'll come tomorrow. I promise."

She hung up and ran downstairs to eat breakfast. To her surprise, her father wasn't in his usual place. "Hasn't Dad come down yet?" Abby asked Coralee.

"The mister ate breakfast early," Coralee replied. "He said he had to work at his office all day today. Whatcha wanna eat?"

"Just cornflakes," Abby said. "And orange juice, if we've got it."

Coralee shrugged. "Go easy on the sugar. My girlfriend said that's one of the first things the Army's gonna take over."

Abby picked up the morning's *L.A. Times* to glance at the news. The Nazis were making strides through Europe. More was revealed about the Japanese capture of islands in the Pacific; one hundred thousand troops had been taken prisoner. Abby shuddered. The Japanese were taking over island after island in the Pacific. Maybe California *would* be invaded.

Even the entertainment section dealt with war. There were stories about stars going on tour to sell war bonds: Lana Turner, Rosalind Russell, Bette Davis. And about stars joining the services: Ronald Reagan in the Army, Jimmy Stewart in the Army Air Force, Tyrone Power in the Marines.

Abby tossed the newspaper to the far end of the table where she couldn't read the headlines, gulped down the breakfast Coralee had brought to her, and left to meet Mary Lou.

At the Red Cross Hut, Abby and Mary Lou worked with a number of other volunteers from Hollywood High School. Soon the conversation spun off into small groups, and over the buzz of voices Abby asked Mary Lou, "How was your date?"

"So-so," Mary Lou said. "He's awfully young."

Abby bent over the cartoon she was cutting out of *The Saturday Evening Post.* "Luke told me that his parents agreed to sign for him." Just saying his name, Abby felt the warmth of Luke's body against hers all over again, and she shivered.

Mary Lou nodded. "I know it's hard on you, but I can understand why he'd enlist," she said. "I would, too, if I were a boy."

"But I keep thinking, what if something happens to him? What if—?"

Mary Lou put her hand over Abby's. "Luke will be all right," she said. "He'll come back safely." When Abby didn't answer, Mary Lou added, "You have to believe that. You can't keep thinking that the worst will happen. It's like—well, like bringing bad luck. You have to have faith."

Abby managed a faint smile. "I'll try," she said, "but you may have to tell me all this again."

"I will. That's what being best friends is all about." Mary Lou reached for one of the pairs of scissors. "After we're through here, let's go over to the Pig 'N Whistle for an ice cream soda."

Abby thought ruefully about her almost empty wallet. "Can't. I'm broke until I get my allowance on Monday."

"My treat," Mary Lou said. As Abby started to shake her head Mary Lou added, "Come on, you can buy me a hot fudge sundae at Brown's next week."

It was close to three o'clock when Abby arrived home. Her mother was in the living room with Mrs. Rice. Abby could hear them laughing.

Abby didn't know why her mother spent so much time with Mrs. Rice. The woman's tiny eyes were constantly probing for new information to pass along with snide insinuations and knowing smiles at her next gossip session.

Abby entered the room and put her books on the nearest end table. "I'm home, Mama," she announced.

Her mother looked up. "Hello, Sweetie!" she cried. Her voice was too loud and her words were beginning to slur. "Be a good girl and say hello to Mrs. Rice."

"Hello, Mrs. Rice," Abby said dutifully.

Mama slowly placed her empty glass on the coffee table, nearly missing it. "It must be lunchtime. I'm getting hungry," she said. "Have you had lunch, Sweetie?"

"A long time ago," Abby said. "It's nearly three o'clock."

"Three? It can't be." Mama squinted, as if she were trying to remember something. "Oh, no!" she said. "I was supposed to pick him up at one."

"You don't mean Bobby?" Abby asked.

"Of course I mean Bobby. I dropped him off at Paramount for an audition. I didn't see any point in sitting around waiting for him, so I came on home. But he was supposed to be through by one o'clock." Mama hoisted herself from the sofa, managed to get halfway up, then lost her balance and sprawled backward.

"You can't drive," Abby snapped, trying with all her will to hold back her anger. "I'll get him."

Her mother's eyes narrowed. "Don't speak to me in that tone of voice, young lady! There's nothing to stop me from driving if I damn well want to!"

"I'm sorry, Mama." Abby forced herself to speak softly. "I just thought I'd get Bobby so you—" she said the first thing that came into her mind "—so you could have a little nap before you get ready for Donald Shaddoe's birthday party."

Mrs. Rice took a last swallow from her glass and put it on the table. "You don't mean Kenneth Shaddoe's son, do you?" A touch of awe had crept into her voice.

"Who else?" Abby's mother answered, looking smug. She gave Mrs. Rice a quick glance. "A nap sounds like a good idea," she said. "I do want to look my best when the limo arrives."

"My, my," Mrs. Rice murmured, as though she were mentally filing the information to repeat somewhere else.

"I'll get your car keys," Abby said, and left before her mother could change her mind.

Abby had no trouble getting onto the Paramount lot. The elderly guard at the gate greeted her happily. "Just like the good old days, Cookie," he said. "You were such a cute little kid, and you always had a wave and a smile for me."

The walk through the lot to the room where auditions had been held wrapped Abby in nostalgia. *This is where I belong,* she mourned. *This is my life.* She passed two dancers dressed like chorus girls and a group of extras in Arabian garb. Tentatively, she smiled at them, but they didn't notice her. Two cowboy extras stopped their conversation to glance at Abby, stared briefly, then turned away, as though she were of no importance and held no possible interest. Her cheeks grew hot with anger and embarrassment.

She flung open the door to the audition room and stepped inside. It was a stark, drab room, bare except for a desk by the door, rows of chipped, wooden folding chairs lining the walls, and a few scraps of paper littering the dusty floor.

Abby groaned. Bobby was gone, and it would be nearly impossible to find him on the huge lot.

A door at the far end of the room stood open, and Abby walked through it into a hall. She heard voices nearby, and she followed the sound.

She entered what looked like a storage room with files across one wall. Kneeling on the floor facing her were two workers in overalls. On the floor between them lay a few crumpled dollar bills and some change. Then Abby recognized the third corner of the triangle, even with his back to her.

"Bobby!" she shouted.

Bobby started, a pair of dice dropping from his

hands. One of the men jumped to his feet. The other reached to scoop up the money, but Bobby flung himself on it. "No you don't! That's mine!" he cried, and shoved it into his pocket.

He stood, giving Abby a beatific smile. "Hi, Abby," he said. "These are two guys I met. They were teaching me a game."

"I know that game," Abby said, glaring at the two men. "It's called 'craps.' " One of the men began to edge past her, but she stepped into his path. "Give back the rest of my brother's money," she said.

"He got it all back," the man said. "Matter of fact, he got some of mine."

"I won it," Bobby said.

"We didn't hurt the kid," the other man said. "We were just havin' a little fun."

"It's not funny! I ought to report you to security."

"Hey, look," he began, but Abby interrupted.

"I think I will," she said.

The man stuck his thumbs into his overall straps and sneered. "You should be glad you found him in here with us. He could have got himself into *real* trouble, left hanging around the lot for a couple of hours on his own."

Abby blushed. There was nothing to say to that. She grabbed Bobby's wrist and tugged him behind her as she strode out of the building.

"Aw, what are you so mad about?" Bobby complained as he struggled to free himself from Abby's grip.

"I'm not mad at you," Abby said, so angry that tears

were running down her cheeks. "I'm mad at Mama. You shouldn't have been left alone."

"Slow down, will you!" Bobby shouted. "I ended up with over three dollars more than I started with. Pretty good, huh?"

They reached the car and Abby finally released him. Rubbing his wrist, Bobby settled back against the seat. "Don't tell Mama," he said.

Abby edged the car out into the traffic on Van Ness before she answered, "You bet I'll tell Mama. This was all her fault."

"How about if we make a deal between us?" Bobby said quickly. "I'll split what I got with you if you keep quiet about the game."

"Don't be ridiculous!" Abby snapped.

For a while he didn't speak, and when he did his voice was heavy with despair. "You're just going to get me in trouble. Mama's going to get mad at me."

"She won't be angry with you. She never is." If anything, their mother was too indulgent with Bobby. Abby had never heard him get scolded.

"She doesn't care about me. All she cares about is you. All she ever thinks about is your career and how you used to be a star."

"Bobby! It's not like that!"

"Yes, it is." He spoke so quietly that Abby almost didn't hear him.

Her voice softened as she said, "Let's talk about something else. How did the audition go?"

"Are you kidding?" Bobby said. "I blew it, as usual. I can't act. Everybody knows that—even Mama."

When they arrived home Abby entered through the kitchen door, Bobby trailing after her. "Did anybody call me?" she asked Coralee.

She held her breath waiting for the answer. Surely Luke would have called. He'd want to make things right again, wouldn't he?

"Nobody called," Coralee drawled.

Abby sighed. "Where's Mama?" she asked.

"Drinkin' coffee," Coralee said. "A whole pot of coffee." She chuckled. "She won't be able to count on that much longer. Soldiers drink an awful lot of coffee."

Bobby disappeared in the direction of the library, while Abby marched up the stairs and knocked at her mother's bedroom door. Without waiting for an answer, she opened it.

Mama sat at her dressing table. In her trembling left hand she held a coffee cup. With her right hand she pressed a damp washcloth to her forehead. "I'm glad you said something about the party," she said in a slurred voice. "That really set Isabel back on her heels. Did you see her face?" She took a quick sip of coffee and grimaced. "I don't know why that one little drink hit me so hard."

Because it wasn't one little drink, Abby thought. But at the moment, that wasn't important. Bobby was.

"You didn't ask me about Bobby," Abby said. She knew her words sounded clipped and tight.

Mama looked up sharply. "Bobby? The audition went well? He got a callback? Tell me. Quick!"

"No," Abby said. "He didn't. But he's home safely— this time, at least."

"What are you babbling about?" Mama asked.

Abby sat on the edge of the bed, across from her mother. "When I got to the studio, no one who had anything to do with the auditions was there. I found Bobby shooting dice with some guys in a back room. He shouldn't be left alone at auditions or when he's working. He's just a boy."

"So he learned how to shoot craps," Mama said with a chuckle. "That isn't so bad, is it?"

"Mama, he's hanging around the wrong people!"

"Bobby's a good kid," Mama snapped, "and what you told me doesn't seem so awful. First you come running to me complaining about his friends at school. Now this silly story. Are you hoping to get your little brother into trouble? Because if you are, you're out of luck."

Abby clenched her hands into fists. "I'm not trying to get Bobby into trouble. I'm trying to make you realize that you're neglecting him!"

Mama put down the cup and dropped the wash- cloth, her eyes wide. "Me? Neglecting Bobby? I devote my life to you kids, and you have the nerve to accuse me of neglecting him! Why don't you tell me the real reason you're so hot under the collar? You're jealous of Bobby. That's it, isn't it?"

"Mama! I'm not jealous of Bobby!" Abby protested.

"Don't tell me that!" Mama shouted. "You've always been jealous, even when he was a baby and people would say, 'Oh, what a beautiful child!' I saw the sly looks you gave him, Missy!"

"Mama, you aren't listening to me! You left Bobby alone for hours. Anything could have happened to him!"

A deep voice spoke from the doorway. "I could hear the two of you all the way downstairs."

Abby looked up at her father tearfully. "The argument's over now, Frank," her mother said quickly. "I set Abby straight. It's all taken care of."

"Why *did* you leave Bobby alone, Gladys?"

Mama was defiant. "He's old enough not to have his mother with him every minute."

"Apparently not."

"Look, I had things to do. I couldn't just sit and wait a couple of hours."

"Then forget about an acting career for Bobby. It will be easier on both of you. If you were honest with yourself, you'd admit he's not an actor and doesn't want to be. You're just wasting his time and everyone else's."

Abby's mother twirled on the dressing-table stool to face her husband. "That's not true and you know it! Dammit, Frank, you also know that I handle the children better than you do. The argument's over. Do you want it to start up all over again?"

Abby's father's face turned a dark red. "Gladys, if you ever leave that boy alone at an audition again, I'll pull him out of that professional school you've stuck him in." He took a deep breath. "It might not be a bad idea anyway."

For a minute Mama hesitated. Then she shrugged. "All right, Frank. If you feel so strongly about it, I'll stay with Bobby when he's on auditions."

"That's all I ask," Dad said. He pressed a hand to his chest and crossed the room. "Is there any more baking soda in the bathroom?"

"There should be," Mama said. "Don't tell me you have heartburn again."

"A touch. Maybe it's the two jobs. There's a lot of stress."

"It's probably what you're eating," Mama said. "Stay away from those spicy tamale lunches on Olvera Street." She turned back to Abby impatiently. "You'd better start getting ready for the party. We have to leave in an hour."

Abby walked silently to the doorway, but Mama called after her, "I put your clothes out on the bed for you. I had Coralee press your pink taffeta dress."

Abby spun around. "Mama, you don't want me to wear that little-girl dress to this party!"

Her mother looked surprised. "Of course I do! It's your fanciest dress."

"It's bad enough when I'm on stage or—" Abby shuddered. "—or at a premiere. I'd feel like a fool in it at the party. For one thing, it's too tight across the chest."

Mama looked at Abby appraisingly, then shrugged. "We'll take care of that," she said. "We'll bind your breasts."

Abby gasped. Mama raised her eyebrows. "Oh, for goodness sakes, Abby. What do you think women did in the twenties, when flat chests were in style? What do you think they did to Judy Garland when she was in *The Wizard of Oz*? She was seventeen—the same age you are now—and they had to make her look thirteen."

Abby groaned, and Mama's voice turned plaintive. "Oh, Sweetie, please don't fuss about the dress. Don't you know how happy it would make me if you wore it? Don't you?"

Abby managed to nod agreement, then ran to the quiet privacy of her own bedroom.

Soaking in a hot bath helped her relax. All right, she'd wear the dress. She really didn't have a choice, since she didn't have any other real party dress.

After her bath, she dutifully submitted to her mother's supervision as she dressed and applied a light pink lipstick and face power—the only makeup her mother would allow.

Finally, Abby stood before the huge, round mirror that hung over her dressing table. When she saw her reflection, she couldn't help it; her eyes filled with tears. "I'm too old for dresses like these," she murmured.

"Oh, no!" Mama insisted. "Sweetie, it's important to keep you looking the way you used to. This is how everyone remembers you. We can't let them forget little Cookie Baynes."

Abby smiled tentatively. "Who would guess that behind that little Cookie Baynes costume lurks the real

Abby Baynes, who—in less than four years, ladies and gentlemen—will legally be an adult."

She saw a flash of terror in her mother's eyes, but Mama quickly recovered. "Nonsense, Cookie," she said, preening at her own reflection and tilting her head flirtatiously to one side. "You're still a child. Look at me. My goodness, I'm much too young to have a grown-up daughter." She smoothed the delicate, dark blue chiffon skirt of her dress and fingered her pearls. "I do look beautiful tonight, don't I?"

Abby could hear the pleading, frightened note in her mother's voice. "Yes," she answered. "You do look beautiful."

Excitement glittered in Mama's eyes. "We're going to knock 'em dead, Cookie," she said. "This is going to be a party you'll remember all your life!"

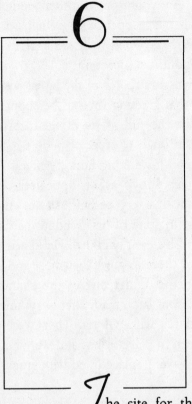

6

$\mathcal{T}$he site for the party was the Shaddoe mansion high up in the hills overlooking the city of Hollywood. It was close to the famous, huge HOLLYWOODLAND sign. The house had been built twenty years before for a romantic leading man of silent films. It was designed like a castle, with stone turrets and small, stained-glass windows. *Everything but a moat*, Abby thought. Colorful banners hung on both sides of the huge front door. The butler who answered was dressed in a gaudy medieval costume. "Right out of the props department," Abby whispered to her mother.

Mama, her face open with delight, quickly hushed Abby. "*This* is Hollywood!" she whispered. "It's what this town is all about! Isn't it wonderful?"

The downstairs rooms of the house were so crowded with people that greetings had to be shouted. Waitresses struggled with the full skirts of their costumes as they maneuvered through clusters of people, passing trays of drinks and mouth-watering hors d'oeuvres.

Al Jerome, Abby's agent, appeared. Abby's mother greeted him with a cry of enthusiasm. Al was tall and good-looking, in spite of his receding hairline. His smile was warm and his eyes twinkled. He kissed Mama, kissed Abby, and led them to greet their host and hostess.

Abby ducked under one of the banners positioned around the room and made her way toward Kenneth Shaddoe and his wife, Gloria. They were dressed as a king and queen in velvet robes and were holding court in front of a massive fireplace filled with sprays of roses and orchids.

Kenneth Shaddoe greeted Abby enthusiastically, taking both of her hands and kissing her cheek. "It's been a long time since I've seen you," he said. "I'm so glad you could come!"

Grateful for his kindness, Abby beamed at him.

His wife looked from Mama to Abby with a puzzled look in her eyes. "How do you do," she said, extending her hand. "I'm Gloria Shaddoe."

Mr. Shaddoe laughed. "Come on, Gloria. Surely you remember this young lady. Cookie Baynes?"

"Why, of course," Mrs. Shaddoe said smoothly. But her words couldn't cover the shock and pity in her eyes as she took in Abby and the dress she was wearing.

Abby felt herself blushing. She mumbled something polite and began to turn away. But Mrs. Shaddoe rested her fingertips on Abby's arm. "The other kids are down in the pool house," she said. "You'll have more fun with them." She pointed. "Just go out the door over there to the terrace. Then it's down the stairs and follow the path to the right. The pool and pool house are right at the end."

She turned to the next guest. Abby looked over at Mama. She was deep in conversation with Al, her eyes sparkling with excitement.

Al smiled broadly. He was having fun, too. Abby knew she was probably the only one at the party who wished she were somewhere else.

Following Mrs. Shaddoe's directions, Abby crossed the room and opened the door.

As she stepped onto the torch-lit terrace and closed the door behind her, she breathed a loud sigh of relief, which was answered by a giggle.

The slender figure of a young woman stepped from the shadows of a potted palm tree and came toward her. "Cookie, is that you?" she asked.

Linda Larkin was dressed in a white cotton off-the-shoulder dress, a flower tucked behind one ear, her dark hair swinging around her shoulders.

Someone else stepped out of the shadows and quickly joined them. "Hi, Abby," he said. "It's just me, Johnny. "So you escaped that mob in there, too."

"Mrs. Shaddoe said I should go down to the pool house."

Linda made a face. "It's full of obnoxious little kids. There are even a magician and clowns, all dressed like jokers, if you can believe it."

"Not jokers—court jesters," Johnny said. "Don't you know your history, Linda?"

Linda shrugged lazily. "Casting directors don't ask if you've passed history," she said. Her dress slipped off her right shoulder. Abby saw the flicker in Johnny's eyes and knew that she wasn't the only one who had noticed.

"I'll walk down there anyway," Abby said. "I didn't mean to interrupt you."

"Fine," Linda said. "You just do that, Cookie."

But Johnny said, "Let's all go down to the pool. We can sit at the far end and talk. It's been a long time since we've had a chance to really talk, Abby. There's a lot to catch up on."

Linda took Johnny's hand possessively as they walked down the lighted path to the pool. "How interesting of you to come in your costume," she said to Abby. "I heard that you wear it for your club appearances—as well as at premieres." She unsuccessfully tried to suppress a giggle. "It's cute. Is it supposed to be a parody of the old days?"

Abby refused to let Linda hurt her. She smiled. "No. I heard they were holding a Cookie Baynes look-alike contest, and I'm hoping to win."

"You'll always be a winner to me," Johnny said. He winked at her, then deliberately changed the subject. "Judy Garland's here. Did you happen to run into her?"

"No," Abby said.

"I heard that she's going to sing for us later." He laughed. "You know how it is at these parties. All of us pros in one place at one time, fighting for center stage."

They walked to the opposite end of the pool—as far as possible from the pool house, which was reverberating with noise—and settled into three of the deck chairs.

"Maybe Cookie will do her little act for us now," Linda said. "She's all dressed for it. 'Good Ship Lollipop,' wasn't it? Oh, no. My mistake. That was Shirley Temple's song."

"It's too bad you didn't have one," Abby said. "As I remember, you never could hold a tune."

Johnny took Abby's hand. "Linda was just trying to be funny," he said, "but she never was very good with a comic routine, either." He laughed, and Abby had to smile.

"Don't talk about me as though I'm not here." Linda pouted as she leaned toward Johnny, the ruffled neckline of her dress slithering provocatively down her other shoulder.

Abby couldn't resist. Pretending to flick ashes from a cigar, she leered at Linda and said, in her best imitation of Groucho Marx, "Yes, indeed, it's very hard *not* to notice that you're here in *that* dress." She leaned toward

Linda. "My first impression was that you were not all there, but a few more shrugs of your shoulders, and I think I'll be proved wrong."

Johnny exploded into laughter, but Linda looked furious. "Just what do you think you're up to?" she demanded.

"Obviously not what *you're* up to," Abby said.

"Stop that! Right now!"

Abby grinned, and in her normal voice said, "Wrong. That's Johnny's line. Didn't I hear him say that when you were in the bushes?"

"That's enough!" Linda actually stamped her feet. "Johnny! You stop laughing at me!"

Just then, a voice from the path above them silenced them all. "Cookie? Abby? Where are you?"

Abby jumped when she heard her mother's voice. "I'm down here at the pool," she called.

"Well, come here! Hurry up!" Mama's voice was shrill with excitement. "We're going to have some entertainment, and I managed to get you included!"

Abby groaned and put her hands over her face. "Ohhh, I can't! I can't!" she cried.

But suddenly her hands were gripped by Johnny's. "Take a deep breath," he whispered.

As Linda shrieked, Abby found herself sailing through the air with Johnny, landing with a splash in the cold water of the pool.

Gasping and sputtering, she fought her way to the surface. Johnny was there, grinning at her. As they treaded water, he said, "What a pity. Your dress is a mess. You can't possibly perform."

Linda's scream had been heard inside the pool house, and many of the younger guests had rushed outside. Now they were leaping into the water, too, laughing and yelling.

Mama's expression, as she stared down at them from the edge of the pool, was a blend of horror and bewilderment.

"I pushed her, Mrs. Baynes!" Johnny yelled. "Come on in. Join us!" He made a swipe toward her ankle.

Mama frantically backed away from the edge. "W-Why?" was all she could manage to say.

"Jumping into the pool is the latest fad at parties. Everybody does it. It's fun," Johnny called. "Maybe Hedda Hopper will write about this escapade. I'll give her Abby's name."

"But—but Cookie's performance—" Mama stammered. She looked from Johnny to Abby.

"Next time, Mama," Abby said. "You don't want people to say I was all wet!"

With an appreciative grin at Abby, Johnny hoisted himself out of the pool, held down a hand, and pulled her from the water.

She shivered, wrapping her arms around her shoulders. The night air was cold, and the water running down her back and legs was freezing.

Some of the guests were hurrying down to the pool now. A few ordered their children out of the water; others only laughed. A rotund comic did a noisy belly flop into the pool, and his girlfriend jumped in after him.

"Hurry! Get into the pool house," Johnny told Abby.

"You can change clothes." He grinned. "They've got robes in there, and you may as well get one before they're gone."

Abby paused to touch his hand. "Thanks," she whispered.

After the party, Mama was somewhat mollified by the hope of publicity in Hedda's column, enough so that she wasn't angry at Abby for the escapade. And Abby was secretly delighted that one of her horrible dresses was totally ruined.

Early Sunday afternoon Mrs. Fitch telephoned. "I was afraid you'd forgotten me. I have something important to tell you," she said mysteriously.

When Abby arrived a few minutes later, Mrs. Fitch told her she'd seen the signal lights again and had called Mr. DeMille.

"He was very polite," she said, "but he doesn't believe me." She lowered her voice. "Now I'm a little suspicious of Cecil himself."

Abby stood with Mrs. Fitch at the window where she'd seen the lights. "I think I know what caused the lights to turn off and on again," she said, and pointed. "See those trees? There, just beyond the Wilmans' house. If it's the least bit windy, those big branches would wave in between you and the downstairs window of the brick house. That makes it look like the lights are flicking on and off."

Mrs. Fitch's lips puckered into a pout. "That's just what Cecil said."

"We may be right," Abby told her. "Have you asked Jiro to take a look?"

Mrs. Fitch sighed. "He says the same thing. Oh, I suppose I'm just a frightened old lady." She wandered over to an overstuffed chair and settled into it. Her large hair bow flopped over one eyebrow. "But there's so much to be frightened of," she murmured.

Abby sat on the footstool next to her and took her hand. "Don't be afraid, Mrs. Fitch. We're perfectly safe."

"For how long?" Mrs. Fitch asked. "Until the Japanese decide to bomb L.A. or invade the California coast?"

"We've got the Army and Navy to protect us," Abby insisted, wishing she felt as confident as she was trying to sound.

"Like they did at Pearl Harbor?"

"That was a sneak attack."

"Any attack would be. No one sends out information bulletins in advance."

Abby pretended to hold a microphone. Imitating the nasal voice of the famous Hollywood gossip columnist Louella Parsons, she drawled, "I have a special surprise for all of you *adorable*, loyal listeners to my radio program. After the sneak preview tonight of that perfectly dreadful new MGM film starring Errol Flynn—naughty, naughty Errol—the Japanese will hold a sneak event of their own. They've sent me a lovely, *exclusive* engraved invitation to a very special sneak attack on the Ocean Park amusement pier. Well! We can tell those Japanese soldiers right now, they may think they're going on a wild ride on the carousel, but we're going to make sure they end up in the fun house!"

As Mrs. Fitch laughed, Abby jumped to her feet and carefully moved the footstool and a small table out of the way. With her imaginary microphone still in hand, she continued her wild broadcast until Mrs. Fitch was laughing so hard that she had to wipe tears from her eyes.

"That's wonderful!" she said. "Where did you learn that routine, Abby?"

"I usually make them up," Abby said. "Do you remember the comic Rusty Drew? He taught me some of his routines, and showed me how to make a routine work."

"Your timing was perfect, and the way you roll your eyes—did he teach you all those techniques?"

"Oh, yes," Abby said. "Rusty was wonderful. He was a good friend of mine."

Mrs. Fitch leaned forward. "Forget those little-girl acts you do, Abby," she said. "You've obviously got a wonderful sense of comedy. *Do* something with it."

Abby shrugged. "I don't think there's any market for material like mine."

"Of course there is, if you just find it. You must believe in yourself. You made yourself a star once. You can do it again."

"Oh, no," Abby said. "That was all Mama's doing. I wouldn't have had a career at all if it weren't for her. And she thinks comedy is 'coarse and unladylike.' "

Mrs. Fitch's thin, knobby fingers clutched Abby's hand and held it tightly. "Listen to me, girl. No matter how hard your mother worked for you, if you hadn't had the talent, you wouldn't have become a star. That talent is something that is strictly yours, and not your mother's doing. Right now neither your mother nor your agent is doing a thing to help you. You have to make some decisions and plans yourself."

"That's just about what Mary Lou told me," Abby said. "She told me I needed to find another agent."

"Mary Lou's a smart girl," Mrs. Fitch said, adding petulantly, "even though she hasn't come to visit me for weeks."

"I'll bring her soon," Abby promised, smiling.

"Fine. And do what she told you. Find another agent."

Abby took a long breath, slowly shaking her head. "Mama isn't going to like that idea."

Mrs. Fitch's clear blue eyes were penetrating. "Don't you think you're old enough to take some action on your own?"

"I—I'll talk to Mama," Abby said. "At least I'll ask her what she thinks."

On the way home, as she walked down the hill, Abby rehearsed what she would say to her mother. She was relieved to find her mother sitting out on the patio reading the *Los Angeles Times*. Good. She could bring up the idea while she still had enough courage to do so.

Abby plopped into the nearest lawn chair. "Mama,"

she began, "I've been thinking about something that might help my career."

Mama dropped her paper. "What's that?" she asked.

"Sometimes," Abby began carefully, "actors have helped their careers by moving to a different studio or signing with a different agency." Mama's eyes narrowed, but Abby had come this far, so she stumbled on. "Al's very nice, but those dates at women's clubs he gets me aren't helping me a bit. Maybe if I had a different agent who could evaluate my career in a different way—"

"That's out of the question, Abby," Mama said calmly. "Who's trying to turn you against Al Jerome?"

"Nobody," Abby said. "I've just been thinking—"

"That kind of thinking is silly." Mama glanced up the hill in the direction of Mrs. Fitch's house. "It isn't hard to put two and two together," she said. "Mrs. Fitch is trying to put ideas into your head, isn't she?"

"Mama! Don't blame Mrs. Fitch!"

"She's senile, Abby. She lives in a fantasy world." Mama got up and walked to the French doors. "If you want to confide in someone, that's what a mother is for," she said, opening the doors. "Don't waste your time with that troublemaking Mrs. Fitch." She walked into the house, shutting the door on Abby and their conversation.

Abby sat quietly for a few moments, not knowing what to do next. She had expected her mother to be a little angry, but she hadn't meant to make Mama jealous or hurt her. She should have spent more time trying to work out a way to broach the idea.

No. If she hadn't spoken up right then, while she

had the courage to do so, she wouldn't have been able to talk about it to Mama at all. Yet without Mama's help, she would never make it anyway. Mama had worked hard to get Abby noticed by the right people, and Abby had become a star.

I can't imagine becoming successful if Mama isn't behind me, Abby thought. *But I can't keep acting like a little girl. I'm not succeeding at that anymore, either. What am I going to do?*

Bobby opened the French doors just wide enough to stick his head through, and yelled, "Telephone, Abby!"

"Is it Luke?" Abby asked, a catch in her voice.

"Uh-uh. It's Mary Lou."

Abby went to the phone in the breakfast room, satisfied herself that Mama wasn't within earshot, and confided in Mary Lou what had just happened.

"Your mother may not have liked the idea, but she didn't actually say you couldn't talk to another agent," Mary Lou told her. "What harm would it do just to talk to Mr. Harkins? It's like asking a doctor for a second opinion."

"I don't know. Maybe," Abby murmured.

Mary Lou warmed to the subject. "If Mr. Harkins does offer to handle your career, if he does have a part in mind for you—something better than those awful club dates—then your mother ought to be really happy. Isn't that right?"

"I—I guess she would."

"Okay, then," Mary Lou said. "Take my advice. Take Mrs. Fitch's advice. Tomorrow, call Mr. Harkins's office and make an appointment. Will you do that?"

The receiver was moist in Abby's hand, and she found it hard to breathe. Defy Mama? But as Mary Lou had pointed out, her mother hadn't actually forbidden her to talk to another agent. And Mama would *have* to be happy if the meeting led somewhere. She'd be grateful in the end if Abby got her own career back on its feet.

"All right," Abby whispered into the phone. "Tomorrow. I'll do it."

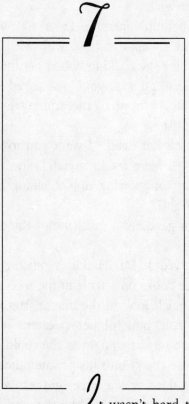

*I*t wasn't hard to get an appointment with Simon Harkins after Abby identified herself as Cookie Baynes. Mr. Harkins's office was in the Security First National Bank building on Highland Avenue. It was a block from the high school, so Abby made the appointment for three-thirty, when classes would be over.

Luke wasn't at school, and Abby missed him terribly. Was she going to lose him? She tried not to think of his arms around her, his mouth on hers. But she yearned to be with him again.

Mary Lou didn't mention Luke. She was delighted that Abby had an appointment with Mr. Harkins, and she did everything she could to bolster her friend's courage.

"Want me to go with you?" she asked as they stood on the sidewalk in front of the administration building after their last class.

Abby shook her head. "I want you to, yes. But this is something I'll have to do myself." She tried a shaky smile. "It's part of growing up, of taking a part in my own career. Right?"

Mary Lou gave her a quick hug. "Knock 'em dead," she said.

Abby arrived at Mr. Harkins's office right on time. She placed her books on a table in the reception area and paused for a quick look in the mirror. Her warm cheeks reflected the pale pink of her sweater. Taking a deep breath, she stood up as straight as she could and followed Mr. Harkins's secretary into his private office.

Simon Harkins was a large, impressive man with a thick shock of white hair. He came around his desk and shook Abby's hand vigorously. His secretary quietly withdrew, shutting the door. "You're a lot taller than the last time I saw you," he said to Abby. "You've been busy growing up." He ushered Abby to a deep, leather chair.

He dropped into his own chair and leaned toward her, resting his elbows on the desk. "What brings you here?" he asked. For the first time Mr. Harkins was silent, waiting for Abby to speak.

With his attention so intently focused on her, Abby forgot everything she had planned to say and stammered, "I—I'm not g-getting parts." She added quickly, "Of course, you must know that."

He nodded abruptly. "Let's get to the point. *Exactly* why did you come to see me?"

Abby forced herself to sit back and try to relax. "Mr. Harkins," she said. "A few years ago, at a party, you told me I had a great deal of talent."

"That's right," he admitted.

His answer encouraged her. "I still do. But I'm not little Cookie Baynes any longer, and I can't keep playing that part. I want to do something else. I desperately want to get back into making films."

He swiveled his chair so that he was no longer facing her as he spoke. "You know," he began thoughtfully, "it's very difficult to make the transition from child star to adult actress. The public keeps thinking of you as—"

Abby interrupted. "But I'm a good actress. Look . . . let me prove it. Please let me read for you. Or let me do one of my routines."

"I've seen your routines," he said. "I don't think I missed a single one of your movies!"

"They're not my little-girl routines! Mr. Harkins, please give me a chance. Let me show you what I can do."

He turned back to face her, his thick eyebrows dipping into a scowl. "I haven't got the time," he said.

"Not even five minutes?"

"Not even that."

Abby knew that the despair she felt showed on her face, because his expression softened, and he asked, "Do you want the truth?"

"Of course I do," Abby said.

"Then I'm going to be brutally honest with you. Frankly, there are three strikes against you. Whether or not you have talent doesn't make any difference, because you haven't got the body or the beautiful face. When you're down on the boulevard, just look around you. Hollywood is filled with young girls with great bodies and gorgeous faces, many of them talented, all of them looking for a chance in films."

Abby wanted to run from the room, but she had asked for the truth, so she held her ground, looking Mr. Harkins right in the eye without flinching.

He paused a moment to assess her reaction, then continued. "To make everything even worse for you, you're typecast, honey. In the mind of every producer in town you'll always be little Cookie Baynes. Sure, you may have been a star, but now they think of you as a has-been."

Abby gasped. His words were like a physical blow.

"Heard enough?" he asked.

Abby stubbornly lifted her chin and stared at him. "You said there were *three* strikes. You've only told me about two."

"Okay." He shrugged. "The third is simply that you're the wrong age. There are very few parts for teenagers, and MGM has a whole stable of kids like Mickey Rooney, Judy Garland, Donald O'Connor, and Jane Powell, whom they've spent years grooming for these roles. The other studios have their favorites, too. Diana Lynn at Universal, Linda Larkin at Fox. Want me to go on?"

"No," Abby murmured. Defeated, she sank back into the soft leather chair.

Mr. Harkins smiled sympathetically and heaved himself out of his chair. He walked around the desk and stood next to Abby, who managed to get to her feet. "You want some advice from me, honey?" he asked. "It's this. Give up your pipe dreams about being in movies again. Forget them. You haven't got a chance. Go to secretarial school. Look around for a Prince Charming. Get married. Raise a family. You'll be a lot happier."

"Prince Charming?" Mr. Harkins had given her the opening she needed. Abby didn't make the mistake of asking again for his permission to perform. She shifted her hips, let her hair fall over one eye, and in a Brooklyn accent went into her act.

"Don't try to tell me—Snow White—about Prince Charming," she said. "What's so great about some guy in a funny suit who comes riding through the forest, gives a perfect stranger a kiss and wants to take her home to mother? Right away I shoulda figured he wasn't too bright."

Mr. Harkins didn't tell Abby to stop. He listened, laughing loudly throughout her short act. When she had finished he said, "Honey, that was great."

Abby could hardly breathe. "Thanks," she managed to say. "I'm glad you liked it."

He shrugged as he regained his composure. "Sure I liked it, Abby, but as I told you, you're not marketable. If you were, I'd take you on in a minute. My advice still stands, and I hope you remember it."

Moving as though she were an automaton, Abby followed Mr. Harkins to the door and walked down the long hallway. There was a strange buzzing in her head. Give up? Plan a future away from Hollywood and the studios? She had never even contemplated it. She couldn't imagine what it would be like. Her entire life had been devoted to a career in the movies.

She stopped in the outer office to pick up her books. The people who were seated in the room, waiting for their appointments, momentarily lowered their magazines to study her, then went back to their reading.

Abby ignored them, but she couldn't help listening to the secretary, who was on the phone. She was obviously talking to one of Mr. Harkins's clients, giving her the time and date of an audition at Twentieth Century Fox. "It's a small part, but a darned good one," the secretary said. "Dress to the teeth. They want a sophisticated, somewhat sultry young woman."

Abby grimaced. Sophisticated and sultry—and undoubtedly possessing "the body" and "the looks." It hurt to remember Mr. Harkins's words. Abby ran down two flights of stairs to the lobby of the building, where she knew she'd find a pay phone. She had promised to report to Mary Lou, and she'd never be able to do it at home, where someone might overhear what she said.

Mary Lou answered on the first ring. After Abby had recounted the entire interview, there was a moment of silence before Mary Lou said, "The man is an idiot. A *rude* idiot."

"He was only being honest."

"He doesn't know what he's talking about."

"That's not what you said when you wanted me to go to see him."

"I wish I hadn't," Mary Lou said. "I had no idea he'd be so cruel. I didn't know he'd try to discourage you."

"I don't know if he succeeded in discouraging me or not," Abby said. "I hurt too much to think about it."

Mary Lou's voice rose a notch. "Maybe you don't even need an agent. Look at Lana Turner. She was discovered by a casting director while she was having a milk shake in Currie's, right across the street from school!"

Abby gave a rueful laugh. "Lana Turner and I don't have much in common. 'The body,' 'the good looks.' Remember?"

"That's crazy!" Mary Lou said firmly, "Abby, don't give up. Besides, you'd make a terrible secretary. You never have been able to spell."

A woman with two small children came up to the phone booth and stared inside. The woman pointedly looked at her watch.

"I'll talk to you tomorrow," Abby said to Mary Lou. "Someone's waiting to use this phone." She paused. "Thanks for listening."

She opened the door to the booth and barely managed to get out before the woman and the children squeezed inside. One of the children tromped hard on her left foot, but Abby didn't even notice the pain until much later, after she got home, went to her room, locked the door behind her, and had a long, comforting, solitary cry.

"You look a little pale, Sweetie," Mama said to Abby that evening at the dinner table. "You're not getting sick, are you?"

"No," Abby said.

"Good," Mama said, "because Al's working on something. He thinks there might be a spot for you in it."

Abby put down her fork, alert and hopeful. "A part in a movie?"

"If it was a movie role, believe me, there'd be bells ringing around here. No, it's some kind of a fund-raiser— but a very important one. Al says some of the right people are bound to be there." She said no more about it, and Abby's hopes fell again. Of course it would be just another sparsely attended program at a suburban women's club.

Soon after dinner the doorbell rang. Abby, who was on her way upstairs, ran down the stairs and opened the door just as her mother came into the entrance hall. Luke stood on the front porch.

Abby's heart gave an extra bounce as she took a step toward him.

"Abby," Luke said. "Will you talk to me?"

"Yes," Abby said. She reached out a hand.

Mama came up behind Abby. "Abby didn't mention that you'd be over, Luke," she said. "It *is* a school night, and her father and I discourage dating on school nights. Perhaps you'd like to come back on Friday, instead."

"Mrs. Baynes, I won't be here on Friday," Luke said. "I've enlisted in the Navy, and I have just a few days to get everything together before I have to report to boot camp."

"Oh," Mama said. Pleasure tinged her voice. "So you've come to say good-bye to Abby. Well, in that case, do come in."

As they walked into the living room, her mother hovered near them, so Abby said, "Mama, it's a nice evening. Luke and I are going to sit outside."

She walked with Luke to the patio, firmly shutting the French doors behind them. Still holding his hand, she led him to the lawn swing. They sat close to each other in silence for a few minutes. The bittersweet fragrance of spring lilies mingled with the scents of the early roses and the honeysuckle vine that arched across the walkway to the lower part of the yard. The low-hung moon softened the darkness with pale light. Abby snuggled closer to Luke, taking comfort in the moment, reluctant to let it go.

Luke cleared his throat a couple of times. "I'm sorry about what happened Friday night," he said. "I shouldn't have pressured you. You were right. I shouldn't—"

Abby interrupted, putting her fingertips over his

lips. "And I shouldn't have gotten so angry. I was angry because I was afraid. I felt—I don't know. I've never had feelings like that before, and they scared me."

Luke pulled his hand from hers and put his arms around her, tucking her head against his shoulder. "Abby, after you sent me away I realized how much I love you," he said. "I'm going to miss you. That's the hardest part of leaving."

"Oh, Luke, I wish you didn't have to go!" Abby said.

"So do I. No one wants to go to war, but it's something that has to be done. We have to fight for our country."

"Let's not talk about it. Let's not even think about it," Abby whispered.

Luke tucked a finger under her chin, raised it, and kissed her. Abby clung to him, eagerly losing herself in his kiss.

Suddenly they were spotlighted as the bright patio lights were flipped on.

"So this is what you're up to!" Mama shouted, coming toward them.

Abby and Luke quickly drew apart, stumbling to their feet.

"I—I was just saying good-bye to Abby," Luke stammered.

"Saying good-bye? Is that what you call it? The two of you sprawled all over each other?"

"Mama! It wasn't like that!" Abby cried.

"Are you telling me I didn't see what I saw with my own two eyes?"

"It was just a kiss," Abby insisted.

Mama glared at Luke. "Please leave. And don't come back. I'm not going to allow you to abuse my hospitality with that kind of behavior!"

"That's not what happened, Mama!" Abby cried. Tears rushed to her eyes.

Luke didn't answer Abby's mother. He turned to Abby and said, "I'll get in touch with you as soon as I can."

"Oh, Luke!" Abby took a step toward him, but Mama was suddenly between them.

Abby watched Luke walk into the darkness, then heard him start his car and drive to the street. She wished with all her heart that she were with him.

She turned toward her mother. "You shouldn't have talked to Luke like that. What you said wasn't true. He was just kissing me good-bye."

Mama shrugged, and her voice was calm again. "One kiss leads to another, Abby. You're just a child. One day you'll know better and be grateful to me."

"I'm *not* a child!" Abby retorted.

"Of course you are," Mama said in a tone that forbade contradiction. Then she smiled sweetly at Abby and reached out to put an arm around her shoulder. Frustrated too many times in one short day to fight any longer, Abby let herself be led back into the house.

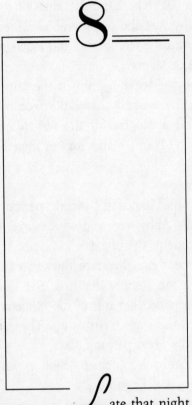

8

$\mathcal{L}$ate that night, as she knelt again at her bedroom window, Abby thought only of Luke. She wanted to be close to him, she wanted his arms around her, she wanted to feel the security of being loved by him. She wished she could shut out the rest of the world.

She loved Luke. She had told him so. This hunger to be held, to be comforted, to be together forever and ever and ever was love, wasn't it? Or was there more?

Shouldn't love be happy? Didn't all the movies end that way? Why was she so miserable? When she thought of Luke why did she feel so hurt and lonely and confused?

Because of Mama?

No. Abby rested her chin in the cup of her hands and sighed. She wished that Luke would telephone so that she could apologize for the way Mama had acted, but she couldn't blame Mama for her mixed-up emotions.

During Miss Standfast's second-period English class the next day, Abby received a message to bring her books and come to the office.

Mama was there, her face flushed with excitement. "You've got a job," she exclaimed. She grabbed Abby's elbow and propelled her out of the office and the building and down the steps. "Hurry up. The car's over here. Lucky I found a good parking place."

"Mama!" Abby complained. "Slow down. You haven't even told me what the job is."

"It's that fund-raiser," Mama said. She threw open the door on the driver's side of her five-year-old black Packard sedan. "Hurry up. Hop in. I'll tell you about it while we're on our way."

Abby reluctantly climbed into the car, noticing as she did one of her puffed-sleeve taffeta dresses laid neatly across the backseat.

"The job's in San Bernardino," Mama said. "It's a

long drive. Anyhow, one of the performers came down with the flu. Al called and asked if you could step in. Of course I said yes. You don't know *who* is going to be there. This may be your big chance." She pointed at the glove compartment. "I brought a bottle of cologne and a box of bobby pins. You can pin-curl your hair right now, and it will be dry when we get there."

Mama rattled on. Abby twirled and wrapped her hair into pin curls, hardly listening. Another of her little Cookie routines! What if she refused to perform? What if she turned to Mama and said, "No! Never again!"

"Mama," Abby said, twisting toward her mother, "I have to tell you something."

But Mr. Harkins's face appeared before her, and his words echoed in her head. "You're a has-been. Give up," he said. "You haven't got a chance."

Mama was waiting for Abby to say something. "What's the matter?" she asked. "Are you cold?"

"No," Abby murmured.

"Well, what is it? What did you want to say?"

"I—I guess it wasn't important."

"Then let's talk about your act," Mama said. "Lately you've been slacking off. You've got to put more sparkle, more pizzazz into your first song. Grab their attention right away. Do you understand what I'm telling you?"

Abby clenched her fists so tightly they hurt. "Yes, Mama," she said.

*   *   *

The dressing room backstage in the old auditorium was scarcely larger than a broom closet. It was hot and it smelled of dust, sweat, and stale cigarettes. Abby shared the room with a woman with dyed black hair who was squeezed into a red, white, and blue satin blouse and matching shorts; a small, black and white terrier who had a red, white, and blue ribbon around its neck; and the skinny, female half of a tap-dancing team.

Mama finished tying Abby's sash into a large bow and backed out of the dressing room. "I'll wangle a seat out front," she said. "Can you get yourself on stage on time? You're on after the dog act."

"I'll be on time," Abby said. Why did Mama even ask? Abby always was in the right place at the right time, without fail, wasn't she?

Abby squeezed to one side of the room to get out of the way of the dancer, who was bending over to tie the ribbon bows on her tap shoes.

The dancer paused to take in Abby and her outfit. "What kind of act have you got?" she asked.

"A medley of songs, a couple of dance routines."

The dancer smiled. "Kind of a parody of the Cookie Baynes and Shirley Temple stuff, huh? It ought to get a good hand."

Eager to change the subject, Abby quickly turned to the other woman and asked the first thing that came into her mind. "Was it hard to train your dog for your act?"

"Naw," the woman said. "Terriers train easy."

"What's your dog's name?"

"Trixie. I used to work with Trixie and her brother

Jack, but Jack just keeled over and died one day, so now there's just the two of us."

Abby reached out to pet Trixie, who sat in a cardboard box on a cushion, but the dog showed her teeth and growled.

"I don't think she'd bite you," the woman said. "She's just gotten crabby in her old age. To tell you the truth, I don't think she sees too good anymore."

Trixie turned in a tight circle three times and settled down on her cushion, her head on her paws. Her mouth was open, and she began to pant.

"I think Trixie is hot," Abby said. "Do you have a bowl? Could I get her something to drink?"

"Not on your life! You can't give food or water to a dog before it goes on stage." She rolled her eyes. "You can imagine what would happen."

A loud rap on the door startled them all. Trixie gave a sharp bark. "Curtain time," a voice called. "First act, take your places."

The dancer stood tall and took a deep breath. "We're on first," she said. "It's a lousy place on the bill. I hate to open."

She threw open the door and hurried from the room. The breath of cool air from backstage was such a welcome change from the stuffy dressing room that Abby decided she'd watch the show from the wings.

The dancers weren't very good, and neither was the magician who followed. His tricks were so old and obvious that Abby thought she could have done them just as well herself, without any practice. He exited the stage to feeble applause, angrily muttering to himself. He glanced at Abby. "Rotten house, kid! Worst I ever had! Don't take it personal."

Abby moved to the slit in the curtain, where she could get a glimpse of the audience. The auditorium wasn't even half-filled. A couple of small children played in the far right aisle, their mother hissing at them to hush. A man in the front row yawned loudly, and two women nearby kept up a mumbling conversation, apparently not bothering anyone except the performers.

The dog act was announced as two stagehands carried a table, standing hoop, and boxes onto the stage. The woman in red, white, and blue ran past Abby and cartwheeled to center stage, Trixie trotting after her.

Trixie looked tired, but her trainer made up for it in enthusiasm. She carried on a light banter, but the audience didn't laugh at her jokes. Then she put Trixie through all her paces, but the audience still didn't respond at all.

Finally, with a "Thank you, thank you, all!" the woman picked up Trixie and bowed off the stage. She paused as she passed Abby and placed a hand on her arm. "Bad house," she whispered. "Don't let 'em get to you."

The piano player, seated in the orchestra pit, banged out the familiar chords from Abby's music on his old upright piano, and the announcer shouted into the microphone, "It's Cookie Baynes!" Abby put a sparkling smile on her face and ran on stage.

A few elderly women leaned forward eagerly and

stared at Abby with surprise, then turned to each other and whispered. One of the children running in the aisle tripped and fell, wailing loudly as his mother struggled to hold him on her lap. The yawner yawned again. The two women deep in conversation didn't miss a beat. Abby's glance met her mother's. Mama was perched on the edge of her seat, her eyes wide, a smile pasted on her face, her head bobbing up and down.

"I'm your little cookie, cookie . . ." Abby began the song that had been written just for her, tapping out the rhythm as she danced and twirled across the stage, the skirt of her dress flying high. She happened to glance down at the piano player, who had twisted on his stool to stare up her legs.

I can't do this any longer, she thought. *I hate being here. I hate this audience. I hate Mama for making me perform. What if I shouted at all these people that they were rude and awful? What if I just ran off this stage?*

But her mouth kept reciting the lyrics of the songs, and her feet kept dancing. Like a windup doll, she finished her act. There was a smattering of applause, a little more than the other acts had received, Abby thought, but she didn't even care. All she wanted to do was get out of that horrible place.

She quickly threw on her school clothes, swooped up her performance outfit, and ran out of the dressing room, nearly colliding with her mother, who was tucking the familiar white envelope into her purse as she came backstage. "They could have paid more," Mama complained. "You got the best hand. Did you hear them,

Cookie?" She began to cheer herself up. "They clapped louder for you than for anyone else! I'm so proud of my good little girl. You really know how to entertain!"

Abby put a hand on her mother's arm. "That wasn't entertainment, Mama," she said.

Mama's eyes opened wide. "Of course it was."

"No." Abby shook her head. "Entertainment means giving people something so wonderful that they stop in their tracks to enjoy it." She gulped back tears. "I care about what I give my audience, Mama. You understand, don't you?"

"No," Mama said, her voice low with hurt. "I don't. Don't you appreciate what I'm doing for you, Baby? The sacrifices I've always made?"

"I appreciate you, Mama." Abby let out a long sigh. Her mother hadn't heard a word she'd said. "Come on," Abby said. "Let's get out of here. I just want to go home."

For the next two days, Abby concentrated on her homework and making up the class work she'd missed. Luke didn't call, and Mr. Harkins's stinging words kept buzzing through her mind. She tried to concentrate on the routine of schoolwork and shut out everything else.

On Friday, Abby's homeroom teacher read a special bulletin. Students were asked to volunteer to write each week to men in uniform overseas. Slips of paper with names and addresses on them were handed out to all the students who raised their hands.

"I feel kind of strange writing to someone I don't

know," Abby said to Mary Lou. She studied the name on the slip of paper she was holding. "I wonder how old this guy is, and what he's like."

"We'll find out when we write to them," Mary Lou said. "And we can let them know right away what we look like. I'll bring my camera to your house tomorrow. We'll take pictures."

"Good idea," Abby smiled. "I'll wear my blue sweater. I wish we could take pictures in color."

Mary Lou shook her head. "They won't want pictures of us in our usual sweaters, skirts, and saddle shoes. Let's wear our shorts and bandanna halters and take some glamorous poses. We might be somebody's pinup picture."

They both giggled, and Abby lowered her voice. "How about sneaking through that break in the hedge around W. C. Fields's house to pose by his pool with the water lilies?"

"Great," Mary Lou said. "I'll bring a lot of makeup. We can comb our hair like Jane Russell's!"

"In *The Outlaw*?" Abby laughed out loud for the first time in many days.

When Mary Lou arrived that afternoon, Abby was ready. She had on a pair of white shorts and a red bandanna, which she'd tied around her neck and waist to make a halter. "Mama, we're going outside to take some snapshots," she called. Then the two girls hurried up the hill to Mrs. Fitch's house.

Mrs. Fitch was delighted to help with their makeup. She watched as Abby applied a bright red lipstick.

"No, no, no," Mrs. Fitch said. "Put your lipstick on last. Concentrate on the eyes. The eyes are the most important feature." She gave Abby a tissue to wipe off her lipstick and began to supervise. Mary Lou had brought the latest Max Factor shade in pancake makeup. They wet sponges and applied it carefully, along with blue eye shadow and black mascara.

"A touch of rouge—just a touch," Mrs. Fitch said. She turned Abby toward her and reached into the makeup case. "Hold still," she said. "Close your eyes. Now stretch your lips. That's right."

She took the bobby pins from Abby's hair and picked up the hairbrush. "We'll part this over on the left side, so it will fall over the right side of your face, and see what happens," she said.

Finally she stepped back. "My goodness!" she said. "I think we overdid it. You look ten years older."

Abby turned to the mirror and gasped when she saw her reflection. The face looking back at her was still not beautiful, but it was glamorous and sophisticated.

Mary Lou beamed at Abby's reflection. "You don't look like Jane Russell," she said. "You look more like Hedy Lamarr. You're . . . what's the word I'm looking for? I know—*sultry*!"

Satisfied with their new looks the girls ran next door and slipped through Mr. Fields's hedge. They took turns posing on the steps to the pool or leaning against the narrow trunks of the palm trees that bordered it and snapping photographs.

Suddenly Fields's front door opened, and the rotund comic appeared on the porch, holding the door frame for support. He shouted, "Get out of my yard, you little—!" The rest of the sentence was so slurred Abby couldn't catch the words, but she caught the meaning all right. She and Mary Lou ran back through the hedge and down the hill. They didn't pause until they flopped on the Bayneses' patio swing, gasping for breath and laughing as though they'd never stop.

Abby held up the camera. "I wonder how these snaps will turn out," she giggled.

"Gorgeous," Mary Lou answered. She studied Abby. "You don't know how glamorous you look. You ought to wear makeup like that all the time. You look so sophisticated."

"Sophisticated? I thought you said I looked sultry."

"Both."

"It's funny that you'd say that," Abby said, "because it reminds me of something. When I was in Simon Harkins's office, I overheard his secretary on the phone. She was telling a client that the studio was auditioning for someone sultry and sophisticated. The same words you used."

Mary Lou sat up straight. "Did you hear where and when this audition is supposed to take place?"

"Yes," Abby said. "On Monday."

Mary Lou grinned. "Well? Is there any reason you couldn't show up for it, too?"

Abby sat up, too. Her excitement grew with the idea that was taking shape in her mind. "I could tell the casting people that Al had sent me," she said. "I'd probably get away with it."

"Can you cut class?"

"Easily," Abby said. "And Bobby's got an early-morning audition on Monday at Warner's. Mama will be going with him, so I'll have no problem getting out of the house."

"Are you sure?"

After the scene with Dad, Abby was positive her mother wouldn't leave Bobby alone for a moment this time. "I'm sure," she said.

"You'll be just what they're looking for—sultry and sophisticated. They'll have to give the part to you."

Abby smiled at the confidence Mary Lou had in her. She understood better than Mary Lou did the fierce competition in Hollywood for any kind of a part. But this audition would give her a chance to break away from the little-girl roles. She'd had plenty of experience at cold-reading a script, and she knew she could do it well. This audition might be just the break she'd been hoping for to launch Abby Baynes's brand-new career.

"You're really going to do it? You promise, you'll go to the audition?" Mary Lou asked.

Abby gave one quick glance toward the house. Mama wasn't in sight or in earshot. "Yes," she said. "Yes, I'll go."

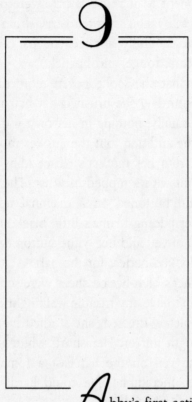

9

Abby's first acting job Monday morning was to fake a stomachache, so her mother would call the school and give her an absence excuse. She was almost too convincing.

"Now what should I do?" Mama worried. "I promised your father I'd stay with Bobby, but if you need someone to take care of you—"

Abby quickly interrupted. "Coralee will be here if I

need anything. I'm not that sick. Go ahead with Bobby. I'll be all right."

The moment Mama and Bobby were out the door, Abby pulled Mary Lou's makeup case from the back of her closet and carefully applied the pancake base, eye shadow, mascara, rouge, and lipstick.

Satisfied that she looked even more dramatic than she had on Saturday, she brushed her hair the way Mrs. Fitch had. Naturally, nothing in her own wardrobe would be right for the audition, but the answer to that problem was simple. From her mother's closet Abby took a two-piece black suit with a nipped-in waist. The jacket had a high neck and buttoned on a diagonal up to the left shoulder. After adding Mama's little black and white hat with the wisp of veil and her white button earrings, Abby thought she looked perfect for the part.

Her mother's high-heeled shoes were somewhat snug, but Abby didn't have any trouble walking in them. When she was completely dressed, she studied herself critically in the full-length mirror. Her short, white gloves looked crisp, and the veil on the hat cast a romantic shadow over her eyes. Incredible! She could hardly believe she was looking at Abby Baynes.

She picked up her handbag, ran down the stairs, and shouted to Coralee, "I'm better now, Coralee! I'm leaving."

"You sure you're well enough for school?" Coralee's voice was coming closer.

"I'm fine!" she yelled, and dashed out of the house before Coralee could catch a glimpse of her.

At the corner of Western and Hollywood boulevards, Abby caught a taxi. She'd spend a good part of her week's allowance on the cab ride, but it would take too long to get to the RKO studio by bus.

When she arrived, she signed in at the gate and was directed to a nearby building. At least twenty women had already gathered in the waiting room. All conversation stopped as every one of them turned to give Abby an appraising glance. She stood near the doorway, as stiff as a bug displayed on a pin; but to her relief the door opened again, another woman entered, and all eyes immediately left Abby to examine the newcomer.

A few minutes later the casting director, a heavyset, balding man, and his two younger assistants entered the room, explained the part, and began handing out scripts.

The hopeful actresses were given a few minutes to go over the lines they were to read, then led to one of the soundstages, where lights were already set up.

Abby settled into one of the canvas director's chairs at the side of the set. She glanced around the huge barn-like building, with its familiar catwalks and miles of cables and lights. The set was a living room, with furniture arranged in front of a backdrop and even a fireplace and windows framed with velvet drapes. Beyond the window was another backdrop with a garden scene.

Abby looked down at her script. The lines seemed a little stiff and stagy, but she did her best with them, reading them over and over, looking for the best emphasis, trying different ways of saying them. It didn't take her long to memorize them.

The first name on the list was called. A plump young woman answered, stood with Keith, an actor who read the other part in the scene, and went through the lines. *She's pretty good,* Abby admitted to herself, *but I can be better.*

One by one they auditioned. A few were asked by the casting director to stick around. Most were thanked and told they could leave. From time to time the director leaned from his chair to say something to the third actress who had auditioned, a dark-haired, beautiful woman who had been told to wait. Had he already made up his mind? That wouldn't be fair! Abby desperately wanted her chance.

Abby grew more nervous as she watched others audition. She was so relieved when they called her name that she jumped too quickly to her feet and stumbled over the legs of the folding chair, sending it clattering to the floor.

She hurried to her spot, but the casting director looked at his watch. "How about we take a lunch break, Eddie?" he asked his nearest assistant, a young, slender guy with a few pimples on his chin and a skimpy mustache much darker than his hair. Abby wondered if he touched it up with mascara to make it more noticeable.

"Oh, no!" Abby blurted out without thinking. She clapped a hand over her mouth.

Eddie took a close look at her, then turned to the director. "We've only got this girl and one other to try out," Eddie said. "Why don't we keep going and get it over with? It won't take long."

Abby smiled at him gratefully, and he winked at her. He smiled, too, as though he were secretly amused. He carefully and slowly studied her, from her hat down to her high-heeled shoes.

Flustered, Abby looked away.

"Okay," the casting director said. "Let's get with it. What's your name, girlie?"

"Abby Baynes," Abby said. It came out little more than a hoarse whisper, and she repeated it.

Eddie caught her eye. His smile became broader, and he winked again. Abby was puzzled. Was Eddie trying to tell her something? Maybe he was trying to give her confidence.

"Well?" the casting director asked her. "How long is it going to take you to get ready—uh—" He glanced at the sheet of names and made a check mark. "—Abby? You've got the first line. Come on. Get going. Read it."

Abby didn't have to read it. She had already memorized the lines. But she jumped into the scene too quickly, nervously stammering over the first sentence. Fortunately, her early training took over, and she moved into the character whose lines she'd learned. She blocked out the people who were watching, as she had learned to do when she was a child, and began to speak the words to Keith the way she felt them. He looked a little surprised that she knew the lines without the script, but he picked up his own pace to match hers, and the scene went well.

"Good reading, honey," the director said. Abby froze, too excited to breathe as she waited for him to tell her to stay. His eyes narrowed as he studied her for a moment.

Then he said, "But don't wait. You're wrong for the part."
He looked at his sheet of names and called the last
woman on the list.

Head down, Abby slowly walked over to her chair
and picked up her handbag. She had tried so hard. She
had to admit that some of the others had been awfully
good, but she had been good, too.

"Don't even bother reading, honey. Wrong type,"
the director told the last tryout. He stood and stretched,
saying to his assistants, "Let's get to lunch before all the
seats in the commissary are filled."

The soundstage was emptying fast, and Abby turned
to leave. But a hand grasped her arm. She looked up to
see Eddie smiling at her.

"Don't look so discouraged," he said.

"I feel discouraged," Abby answered.

"I liked your reading."

"I wish your boss had."

Eddie bent close to murmur, although they were the
only ones left by then. "He'll give you a second chance.
All you need is for me to put in a good word for you."

"But he's already told me I was wrong for the part."

"He can be persuaded. I have a lot of influence with
him. Believe me, I can get you included in the callback."

"I did my best. He didn't think it was good enough."

"There are ways and ways of interpreting a part. You
picked one way, and it didn't work. I'll be glad to go
over the lines with you a few times and show you how to
put more into the part."

Abby was puzzled. "I don't understand."

"It's simple—I think you deserve a chance. Let's get out of this dusty old barn, and I'll show you what I mean." He picked up one of the scripts. "There are a couple of rooms over here where we can work in comfort." He reached for Abby's hand and led her into one of the dressing rooms.

Eddie shut the door, saying, "We'll need a little privacy."

Abby stiffened. "Why?" she asked.

Eddie chuckled and pointed to a stool in front of a dressing table. "Sit down," he said. "Do you want me to help you, or not?" Without waiting for Abby's answer, he added, "For openers, let's get some of that red, red lipstick off." He reached for a nearby box of tissues and put it in her hands.

"It's the latest color."

Eddie shrugged. "But it's too much for now."

"You mean for the audition?"

"Get rid of it," Eddie said.

Abby was hesitant, but Eddie seemed businesslike, so she perched on the stool, facing the mirror, and wiped off her lipstick.

He stood close behind her. "And take that thing off your head," he said.

"That 'thing' is my hat." Abby tried to banter, but her smile was shy and uncertain.

"The hat's one of your problems. It shades your face too much. I want to see what you look like without it." Before Abby could move, Eddie pulled out the hat pin and took off her hat, placing them both on the table beside her. "You're not a raving beauty, but you've got a nice face," he said. "Don't hide it under a hat."

He studied her for only a moment. "Now for the bobby pins. I don't know why women want to wear them." Deftly, he took out the pins and began to fluff out her hair, his fingertips lightly massaging her scalp at the temples. "Like it?" he asked softly.

"What are you doing?" Abby asked. She tried to rise.

But Eddie's hands moved to her shoulders, pinning her down. "Take it easy," he said. "How can I get you to relax if you're so edgy?"

"I—I don't think—"

"Look in the mirror," he said, and smiled. "You've got to get rid of the frown if you want to make a good impression on any casting director—or his assistant."

The expression on Abby's face was so strained that she couldn't help laughing nervously.

"That's it," Eddie said. "You're starting to relax. That wasn't so hard, was it?"

"No." Abby smiled back at him.

For a few moments he massaged the back of her neck, and Abby, beginning to unwind, closed her eyes. Then suddenly, Eddie stooped, encircled her shoulders with his arms, and began to unbutton her jacket.

"Don't do that!" Abby cried, grabbing at his hands. "I can't take off my jacket. I'm not wearing a blouse."

He grinned at her in the mirror, pressing his cheek against hers. "That's the idea, isn't it?"

"No!"

He scowled. "Honey, if you want me to help you, then you've got to give something in return. I don't mind a little of this shy, hard-to-get act. I'm willing to play along for a while. But you've got to start cooperating. That's the way it's done. You understand that, don't you?"

Abby twisted, pulling away from him, jumping to her feet. "No!" she shouted. "I thought you were going to help me."

"You thought I was going to give up my lunch hour just to do a good deed for the day? You're not that naive, are you? C'mon, baby."

Eddie reached for her, but Abby grabbed her handbag and swung it, hitting him on the side of the face.

"Ow!" he yelled, and stepped back.

Abby leapt up and ran to the door. She threw it open and dashed across the empty soundstage, the clatter of her footsteps echoing and re-echoing.

Her heart beating wildly, she ran through the main gate and out to the street, just as a man was stepping out of a taxi. She elbowed past him and jumped inside, giving the surprised driver her home address. As he drove into traffic she gave way to her tears.

While Abby fumbled inside her purse, trying to find her key, her mother opened the door. "I saw the taxi," she said. She gaped as she took in Abby's appearance. "That's my suit!" she exclaimed. "What in the world—?

Look at your face! It's all smeary with mascara! What have you been up to?"

"I thought I'd get home before you did," Abby said as she followed her mother into the living room.

"That's obvious!" Mama scowled. "You couldn't have gone to school like that. You cut school, didn't you?"

"Yes," Abby said.

"You've got a lot to tell me about, Missy," Mama said. "Sit down and get started."

Abby dropped into one of the wing chairs, and her mother sat across from her.

"First of all, what are you doing in my good black suit?" Mama demanded.

The house was unnaturally quiet. "Where's Bobby?" Abby asked.

"Where's Bobby? Is that the only answer you can give me?" Mama snapped. "He's back in school, that's where."

"Oh. I thought his audition would take longer."

"Checking up on me? Well, I'll have you know that Bobby got the part. It's in a Humphrey Bogart movie." For an instant Mama looked smug. "It isn't exactly a speaking part. Bobby will be just one of the neighborhood kids, but he'll be *seen*, and that's important."

"Mama," Abby said, "I was trying to get a part in a film, too."

Her mother's eyes widened. "Dressed like that? That's a laugh!"

"I'm sorry that I borrowed your clothes without telling you," Abby said. "I thought I could come home and tell you I got a part—or even a callback—and it would make you happy."

"Obviously, you didn't get it, because you've been crying. You look like a clown with that mascara smeared all over your face."

"Mama, please!" Abby began crying again. "I need you! I need you to listen to me!"

The expression on her mother's face suddenly softened, and she leaned back in her chair. "Well, of course you do. Go ahead," she said. "I'm listening."

The words came pouring out as Abby told her mother everything. She began with her visit to Mr. Harkins and ended with her flight from Eddie and the studio. When she finished, she leaned back and closed her eyes, drained of every feeling except relief.

"Oh, poor little Cookie," her mother murmured. "See what happens when you don't listen to Mama? I really do know what's best for you."

Abby opened her eyes, grateful that her mother hadn't reacted with anger. "I thought you might be mad at me," she blurted out.

"Mad?" Mama let out a long sigh. "No. I'm not mad. I'm deeply hurt that you'd do a thing like this to me, but I'm not mad."

"I didn't mean to hurt you, Mama."

"I know." She sighed again. "You didn't stop to think about my feelings. You never do." But her face tightened as a new thought struck her. "Where did you get the makeup?"

"I borrowed it."

Mama's eyes narrowed. "From Mrs. Fitch?"

It was tempting to lie, to say she'd bought it, but Abby answered, "No. From Mary Lou."

"Did she know what you were up to?"

"Most of it."

Mama shook her head as though she were shaking off a buzzing fly. "Well, what would she know about the motion picture industry? You're both foolish little girls. What you did *was* stupid, Abby."

"I want to be an actress again," Abby broke in. "I thought I might make it." She leaned forward, intently. "Mama, I've *got* to have a movie career. I've got talent, and I need to be able to use it. Oh, Mama, nobody could possibly know how much all this means to me."

"*I* know," Mama said. "Believe me, I know. Why else would I spend my every waking moment trying to help you? Can't you see what I'm doing for you?"

"Yes, Mama. Of course I see."

"Nobody wants a film career for you more than I do, Cookie."

Abby nodded.

Her mother sighed again. "Now I *am* a little angry," she said. "I'm angry because you value so little all the hard work I've done for you."

"Oh, no, Mama!" Abby said. She crossed the space between their chairs and knelt at her mother's feet, grasping her hands. "I'm grateful to you. Please don't be unhappy with me."

"You just never have appreciated all the sacrifices I make for you." Mama pulled her hands from Abby's grasp, took an embroidered handkerchief from the breast pocket of her dress, and dabbed at her eyes.

"Please don't cry," Abby begged. "I didn't mean to make you cry."

Mama stopped sniffling and stared down at Abby. "Then you're going to have to promise to trust me and not rush off with any lamebrained ideas of your own."

"I thought I was doing the right thing," Abby murmured. "I didn't think my ideas were stupid."

"Well, they *were* stupid. Crawling to another agent! Dressing up like a fool and going to that audition! I'm surprised the director even let you read. And getting taken in so easily by that two-bit casting assistant!" Mama shook her head sadly. "I just hope that Al never finds out how you used his name to get into the studio!"

Mama rose to her feet. "I hope you've learned your lesson, young lady," she said.

"Yes," Abby whispered.

"Good." Mama left the room, and Abby sagged against the seat of the chair, pillowing her head in her arms. "I'm your little cookie . . . cookie . . . cookie . . ." she sang. Cookie Baynes, has-been, with nowhere to go.

10

*M*ama hovered over Abby for the rest of the day, calling her "Sweetie" and "Cookie," pleased to show how forgiving she was willing to be so long as Abby was willing to admit how badly she had gone wrong without her mother's guidance.

Abby wasn't ready to forgive herself, though. When Mary Lou called that afternoon to get the news, Abby didn't want to speak again about what had happened. "It didn't work out," she said. "I had a chance to read, but I wasn't right for the part. At least, that's what the casting director said."

"Lots of parts are going to come up," Mary Lou told her, "and one of them is going to be right for you. Just promise me you won't get discouraged."

Promises. Everyone wants promises, Abby thought. "I guess," she said.

"Do you want me to come over?" Mary Lou asked. "I will. Right now."

"No," Abby told her. "I still have homework. Oh— better tell me what we have to do in English and chemistry."

Abby wrote down the assignments and cut short the conversation. She didn't want to talk to anyone, not even her best friend.

But by evening she felt terribly lonely. Her father hadn't come home to dinner—another meeting of the civil defense committee. Her mother was getting ready to go to dinner and a double feature with Mrs. Rice. Coralee had given notice that she'd stay only two more weeks, so she was in her room, sorting her things, and Bobby was upstairs doing homework and listening to the radio.

Abby didn't want to talk to either Coralee or Bobby, anyway. She finally admitted there was only *one* person she did want to talk to—Luke. Abby missed him so much she could hardly stand it. Where was he? Why hadn't he written? Why hadn't he called?

*   *   *

Three days later the mailman brought Abby a thin envelope addressed in a wavy scrawl with no return address. It had been mailed from San Diego. Luke was in boot camp at the naval base there. When boot camp ended he hoped to get a weekend pass and come north. "No matter what your mother said, I'm going to see you before I'm shipped out," Luke wrote.

At last! That weekend seemed awfully far away, but Abby was willing to wait.

Next to the mail on the hall table lay the evening edition of the *Herald Express*. Abby glanced down at the front page to see the usual stories of bombings, raids, and casualties thousands of miles away. She shuddered, clutching Luke's letter to her chest. The sooner that weekend came and went, the sooner Luke would be involved in all that horror!

The door opened behind her, and she turned to see her father. "Hi, Dad. You're home early," she said.

"I'm skipping the meeting tonight," he told her. He took off his hat and put it on the shelf in the hall closet. "I'm just too tired."

"Can I get you something, Daddy? Would you like some hot tea?"

He put an arm around her shoulders and hugged her as they walked into the living room. "That sounds good, Abby. I *would* like a cup of tea. Make it weak, no sugar. Okay?"

Mama, humming under her breath, trotted into the room, saw Frank, and stopped short. "What are you doing home, Frank?" she asked. "You were supposed to go to a meeting tonight."

"I was on my way, but I changed my mind. They'll have to get along without me," he said. "I'm too tired to add anything worthwhile to the discussion."

"I thought it was important government business, civil defense," Mama said. "How can you miss a meeting like that?"

Abby's father just shrugged. "How about that tea now, Abby?" he asked.

As Abby headed for the kitchen, she heard her mother say, "I made plans for tonight, Frank, and I can't change them. If you had just let me know. You should have telephoned. . . ."

Abby shut the kitchen door. She turned on the gas flame under the teakettle.

As she took out the tea cannister and measured a spoonful of brown leaves into the metal tea ball, she realized how happy it made her to do this for her father. *I don't see much of him these days*, she thought. *I'm glad he's going to be home tonight.*

When the teakettle whistled, Abby poured the water over the tea ball in the pot, put a cup and saucer on a tray with the teapot, and took it in to her father. He was sitting in the den, his coat, vest, and tie off and the collar of his shirt unbuttoned.

Abby poured his tea and sat nearby, watching him. His face was pale, and his eyelids drooped. "You aren't sick, are you, Dad?" she asked.

He shook his head and smiled. "No. Just tired.

Don't worry about me." Gingerly, he took a sip of the hot tea. "Very nice," he added. "Thank you."

For a while they sat in silence, and Abby studied her father. She had always loved him, and she knew he loved her, but he was a man who had never been demonstrative and seemed to find it impossible to make small talk.

He's so different from Mama, Abby thought. *I wonder what they ever saw in each other.*

Just then, Mama swirled into the room, her expensive perfume leading the way. She was wearing the same black suit and hat that Abby had worn to the audition, but she'd added pearls and a pink scarf and looked more beautiful than ever. "I've got to run," she said. "I'm meeting Isabel, and I'm going to be late if I don't hurry."

"Where are you going?" Frank asked. He put down his tea cup.

"Chasen's, I think. We haven't been there for months."

"I thought you and Mrs. Rice had dinner at Chasen's the last time you went out," Abby said.

"I don't know where you'd get an idea like that," Mama said quickly. "I distinctly told you we went to Perino's." She bent down and made a kissing sound at Frank, missing his cheek by a couple of inches. "Next time you plan to come home early, Frank, I'd appreciate it if you'd let me know." Without waiting for an answer, she hurried from the room.

"Mama looks so pretty," Abby said.

Her father nodded. "She's a beautiful woman."

"You and Mama used to go out a lot, I remember. You'd both get all dressed up, and Mama would twirl around like a fashion model so I could see her dress." Abby tilted her head and studied her father. "You haven't gone out together for a long time."

"I've been very busy," he said. He kept his eyes on the cup and saucer that rested in his lap.

"I bet Mama would love to go out with you, Dad," Abby said. "It couldn't be that much fun for her to go out with Mrs. Rice. Why don't you ask her? Take her to something special. Maybe the Palladium for dancing?"

He looked up at Abby and nodded thoughtfully. "Maybe that would be a good idea," he said. "It's just—well—sometimes things become a habit. I guess work has become a habit with me."

Abby sucked in her breath. "Is that my fault, Dad?" she asked.

He shook his head. "Of course not, Abby. Granted, we lived beyond our means while you were on studio salary, but that wasn't your fault. That was our own poor planning. I wish we had banked your entire salary for you, not just what was required by state law."

"I don't care, Dad. You can have everything I make, if you want it," Abby said.

He smiled. "You've already bought us this house, honey, and the cars we drive, and a great deal more. Incidentally, just between you and me, because your mother doesn't know it, the house is in your name, with our signatures only as your legal guardians."

"But—"

"It's only fair," he said. "You earned it." He paused, taking a couple of deep breaths, before he added, "Abby, don't sell this house. Don't let anyone sell it for you or talk you into selling it. People are flocking to Los Angeles because of the war. After the war many of them are going to move here to stay, and property values will keep going up."

For an instant Abby was frightened. "Why are you telling me this? I don't understand."

He smiled. "I don't know why myself. Sometimes I mentally catalog things and put them in order. All habit, I guess." He put his tea cup on the tray. "You can take these back to the kitchen if you want."

Abby picked up the tray and carried it to the kitchen. Dad was all right, she told herself, only tired, as he'd said.

Abby was putting the tea tray back on its shelf when the telephone rang. "I can see those signal lights again," Mrs. Fitch whispered to her. "I suppose I shouldn't bother you, but . . ." Her voice trailed off as she added, ". . . it's terrible to be alone at a time like this."

"I'll come right up," Abby told her. "I'll stay with you for a little while."

She pulled on a jacket and walked up the hill. When Mrs. Fitch answered the door, Abby said, "Come outside with me, Mrs. Fitch. I want to show you something. Put on your coat or a sweater, because the breeze is chilly."

Abby led Mrs. Fitch to the far corner, where Linwood curved into Laughlin Park Drive. They stood between the rows of eucalyptus trees, inhaling the pungent, medicinal smell that came from the leaves and pods, and Abby pointed to the house higher up on the hill. "Do you see the lights now?" Abby asked.

"Yes," Mrs. Fitch said.

"They aren't blinking, are they?"

"No."

"All right. Come with me." She took Mrs. Fitch's hand as they walked back to the driveway of Mrs. Fitch's house. Between where they stood and the suspected brick house were the trees on the Wilmans' property. The branches were moving in the breeze. "Now, take a look," Abby said.

Together they watched the lights blink erratically.

"Tree branches," Mrs. Fitch said.

"Now do you believe me?"

Mrs. Fitch pushed her drooping hair bow into place and said, "Oh, I suppose I believed you all along. It's just so—so frightening in the world now. Sometimes, especially in the dark, it's hard to handle it." She turned to peer into Abby's face. "You're not going home now, are you?"

"I came for a visit," Abby reassured her. "Let's go inside."

Abby settled into one of Mrs. Fitch's dark red over-stuffed chairs. The prickly, plush fabric tickled her bare legs. Jiro brought them cups of hot chocolate with whipped cream on top, but that didn't seem to cheer Mrs. Fitch.

"Inside I'm only twenty," she said, turning a sorrowful glance on Abby, "so it's hard to accept the fact that I'm really a silly old lady."

"You're not silly, and you're not old," Abby said.

"But you are a lady. A very elegant lady."

"Hmmph." Mrs. Fitch snorted. "That's sweet, Abby dear. But 'elegant' isn't exactly what I've ever aspired to. I'll show you the sort of thing Madeleine Perry Fitch was known for in her day."

Revived by her own reminiscence, Mrs. Fitch rose and went into an energetic soft-shoe routine.

"Wonderful!" Abby applauded as Mrs. Fitch ended her show with a perfect curtsy.

Mrs. Fitch, breathing heavily, grinned and lifted her skirt to her thighs. "These are the legs which helped make me famous," she managed to say. "They're still good-looking legs!"

She sank onto the sofa, patting the seat beside her where Abby was to sit. "I used to be a chorus girl," Mrs. Fitch said as soon as Abby was seated. She quickly amended, "Oh, not just any chorus girl. I was a show girl, a member of the Floradora Sextet. We were famous as the six most beautiful singers and dancers in the world, and we knew it. But talent?" Mrs. Fitch chuckled. "I may have been young, but I was practical. I was aware of my own limited abilities and knew that beauty lasts only so long, so I decided what I wanted out of life and set my sights on it."

She paused, then said, "We were wined and dined by wealthy men—even foreign aristocrats. We were encouraged to choose the best of our stage-door Johnnies and marry. And I did. My husband was sweet and adoring and assured me a secure future. In turn, I was a good wife, a beautiful ornament on his arm, and I did what I could to make him happy."

She put a hand on Abby's arm, her fingers pressing for emphasis as she said, "But you can do much better than I did, Abby. You have talent, and you can make a real career for yourself."

In a rush of words, before she lost the nerve, Abby confessed to Mrs. Fitch what Mr. Harkins said and what had happened at the studio audition.

Mrs. Fitch listened sympathetically. "So the part was wrong for you. There were twenty-some young women trying for that part. Remember, only one got it. How do the rest of them feel? Are they all going to give up?"

"But it's different with me."

"How is it different with you? They hurt, too. They can get just as disappointed as you. Oh, Abby, there are many more stories of heartbreak than of success in the acting business."

"But Mama said—"

Mrs. Fitch stubbornly shook her head. "I don't want to hear what Mama says. I want you to believe in yourself, Abby. If you can do that, then you've already won half the battle."

"I couldn't have been a star if it weren't for Mama," Abby insisted.

But Mrs. Fitch snapped impatiently, "A *baby* star. You had the talent, and Mama was there to make sure it got noticed when you couldn't speak for yourself. That's all it amounted to. Sooner or later, Abby, you're going to have to make the decision to stand on your own two feet."

A sparkle suddenly came to Mrs. Fitch's eyes. "I

have an idea," she announced, "and I do believe it's a good one."

"What kind of idea?"

"Don't sound so suspicious. Let me give this a little thought, and in the meantime think about what I've told you." Mrs. Fitch lowered her voice. "And I trust you to keep my past a secret. Not because I'm ashamed of it." She patted her hair bow into place. "It's just that I look quite young for my age, and if people knew I had been in the Floradora Sextet, they'd figure out how old I really am!"

As Abby returned home the phone was ringing again. Her father called out, "Abby, you may as well get it. It's going to be for you. The young man's telephoned every ten minutes since you left."

The young man? It had to be Luke! Please let it be Luke! Abby dashed into the breakfast room and, without turning on the light, grabbed for the phone. "Hello?" she gasped.

"Abby, it's me—Luke." Behind him she could hear voices.

"Oh, Luke! I've missed you! How are you? *Where* are you? What are they doing to you in boot camp?"

He interrupted. "Abby, hold on for a minute. I can't talk long. There's a line of guys waiting for the phone, and I've got something important to say, so just listen. Okay?"

"Okay." Abby sank into the nearby chair and gripped the phone so tightly her fingers were numb.

Luke's voice dropped. "I'll be here at least another three weeks. But I got this idea. When I finish boot camp and some special training stuff I'll get a week-end pass ... What I want to say is ... what I mean is ... oh, Abby, I want us to get married before I go overseas!"

"Married?" The word came out in a whisper.

"Could you find out what we need to do to get a license? Could you find someone who'll marry us? If we have to, we could even drive down to Mexico. . . ."

Abby's heart leapt. She could run away from her problems, run away with Luke and marry him. For an instant she wavered.

But married? "If I hadn't got married and got preg-nant, I could have had a career!" Mama's words sounded loud in her head. "You can do much better than I did. You have talent." Mrs. Fitch's words were just as strong.

"Wait, Luke. Listen!" Abby was shaking so hard it was hard to think, and harder to speak. But Luke was waiting. She had to say something, and she had to say it the right way. "I love you, Luke," she began. "I'm sure that I love you. But I don't want to get married now. We're too young. This is all too fast."

"I'm offering you marriage, Abby. Isn't that what you want?" Luke sounded bewildered.

"I don't know." Abby's voice broke.

"What do you mean, you don't know? You said you loved me. Wasn't that true?"

"Of course it was true," Abby said. "But Luke, I want to be an actress, and if I get married ..." She stopped. Her thoughts were so jumbled she couldn't explain them to herself, let alone to Luke.

His voice was so low she could hardly hear him. "What do you want, Abby?"

"Oh, Luke," she wailed, "I can't make such an important decision so fast."

"Abby," Luke said, "I want us to have something special together before I get shipped out. It means a lot to me. I want it to mean a lot to you, too."

She heard a male voice saying, "Come on. Hurry up. There's a line waiting."

"Take it easy, buddy," Luke said. "Abby? What do you say?"

She couldn't speak. She couldn't think of what to answer. Luke said, "Will you at least think about it, honey? You've got a couple of weeks to make up your mind. Will you promise to think about it?"

"Yes," Abby whispered into the phone. "I will."

"I love you," Luke said.

Abby wasn't sure what she answered. Then Luke said good-bye and hung up.

For a long time Abby sat in the darkness, trying to make sense of her thoughts. Luke was going off to fight, maybe to die. Couldn't she give him what he asked for?

But marriage was supposed to be forever. If Luke came back in a few years—whenever this horrible war was over—would they still be in love? Would they want to spend the rest of their lives together? Abby thought of her mother's wasted dreams and her parents' marriage and put her head down on her arms in despair.

And what about the career she wanted so much? What about her dreams of once again being a star? Suddenly, she was flooded with guilt. Her career—her nonexistent career. Did it really mean more to her than Luke?

Abby sat up and took a deep breath. The answer was, as long as there was a chance left for her as an actress, yes. Even though that chance might be nothing more than the faintest glimmer, she would not let herself lose sight of it. Even if it meant giving up someone she loved—even if it meant giving up Luke.

11

*T*he next day, while Mary Lou and Abby were eating lunch on the lawn at Hollywood High, Mary Lou pulled a drugstore photo envelope from her purse and handed it to Abby. "Take a look at our pictures," she said. "Boy, are they glamorous! You *do* look like Hedy Lamarr."

Abby examined them and smiled. "I wrote to my soldier last night," she said. "I told him something about myself and something about Hollywood. Then I didn't know what to say, so it wasn't a very long letter."

"If he writes back and sounds interesting, you can send him one of these pictures," Mary Lou said. "You might find your pen pal turns into a boyfriend."

"I don't want another boyfriend," Abby said quickly.

"That reminds me," Mary Lou went on. "The nephew of a friend of my mom's is in San Diego. He's a marine, and he wants to come up to L.A. next weekend with one of his buddies in the corps. How'd you like me to fix up a double date? It would do you good to get your mind off Luke."

Abby took a deep breath and blurted, "Luke called last night from San Diego. He wants to marry me."

Mary Lou's sandwich fell into her lap. "He wants to marry you?" she repeated. "Abby! What did you tell him?"

"That I didn't know. But he asked me to think about it."

"What are you going to do?"

"Oh, Mary Lou," Abby began. "He's going away to help fight a war. He might not come back. He—" Her voice broke.

"Do you want to marry him?"

"I'm not ready to get married. We're too young. I might never know if I could . . . " Abby stopped and sighed. "I want to be an actress again. No, not just an actress—a real *star*. I want it so much it hurts. But Luke . . . I love him, and I feel so guilty when I think of hurting him." She looked at her friend pleadingly. "What should I do?"

"I can't tell you that," Mary Lou said. "You're going to have to make that decision yourself."

"I know," Abby whispered. "I'm trying so hard to be fair, both to Luke and to myself, and I'm not sure I'll ever know if I'm doing the right thing."

When Abby hopped off the streetcar at the Harvard Boulevard stop that afternoon, she walked a half-block to the El Adobe drugstore on Kingsley to pick up a package of notebook paper. The small store was crowded with customers, and Abby recognized a few kids from Hollywood Professional School.

She found the three-hole paper she needed and rounded the aisle toward the checkout stand. Bobby—his back to her—was at the end of the checkout line. As Abby smiled and stepped forward to join him, she saw Bobby smoothly take a candy bar from the display and slip it in his pocket.

Without a word Abby slid behind Bobby, reached into his pocket, and pulled out the candy bar.

Bobby whirled around. "Hey!" he gasped in surprise, but his face paled as he saw who was standing behind him.

"Next?" the clerk called, and Abby quickly handed her the package of paper and the candy bar.

"Look," Bobby mumbled, "I—"

"Be quiet," Abby ordered. She collected her change, and marched her brother out of the store. "You promised me you wouldn't," she told him. "If you needed money, all you had to do was ask me."

Bobby shrugged. "Stanley said it was neat to take something and get away with it."

"Stealing is wrong. It's important for you to know that."

"I know what's important," Bobby said. "To get to the top and get what you want. To *be* somebody!"

"To be somebody!" Shivering at the words she'd heard so often before, Abby turned her anger against Stanley. "Where is Stanley?" she snapped. "I'd like to tell him what I think of him."

"I told you," Bobby said. "He isn't here." He looked down and kicked at a pebble. "He said something rotten, so I told him to go jump in the lake."

Abby studied her brother, forcing herself to calm down. He looked pale and sullen. She could tell he was really upset. Finally she said, "Let's walk home. Do you want to tell me what happened?"

They walked together up the broad, tree-lined avenue toward Franklin. Abby, her anger melting into concern for her brother, kept silent, hoping Bobby would confide in her.

"Stanley called Mama a dirty word," Bobby burst out at last. "He said that Mama had a boyfriend. He said a lot of people in this town know it and Dad was dumb because he didn't."

"That's ridiculous!" Abby exploded. "Don't you know Stanley made up all that stuff just to make you mad?" She clutched Bobby's shoulder and stared into his face. "Stay away from Stanley!" she warned. "He's a real creep to invent a rotten story like that, and he's going to keep on trying to get you into trouble, Bobby. He almost did."

Bobby made a face. "I told you. I don't like Stanley anymore."

"Good," Abby said. "He'll probably say other things to make you mad, but don't pay any attention. Stanley doesn't know what he's talking about."

Abby practically sprinted up the hill, breathing hard, trying to exhaust her own anger. Bobby was right on her heels.

When the two of them slammed into the house through the kitchen door, they found Mama on the phone. "Yes, she's here," she was saying. She put her hand over the mouthpiece of the receiver and whispered, "It's that Mrs. Fitch. She said she was at her upstairs window and saw you walking home. Silly old woman to lie in wait for you like a—a vulture!"

Abby shrugged and took the receiver, trying not to appear too eager about the call.

Mrs. Fitch's voice trembled with excitement. "I have wonderful news for you, Abby! Can you come over right now? I want to tell you all about it in person!"

"I'm coming," Abby said. She hung up, said to Mama, "I'll be back in just a few minutes," and dashed out the kitchen door before her mother could tell her not to go.

Mrs. Fitch was waiting for Abby at the gate. She quickly pulled her inside. Clapping her hands together with delight, she said, "In the past I've done a few favors that haven't been returned. This week I called in a marker or two. I've arranged for you to work in a chorus line at a big Sunday afternoon benefit party called *Stars for the USO*. It's going to be held at the Pickfair estate in Beverly Hills."

Abby's heart fell a little. "A chorus line?"

"It's a start," Mrs. Fitch said. "It's something more than the little-kiddie things you've been doing. You won't be cute Cookie Baynes. You'll be grown-up Abby. You can learn the steps quickly with your dance background, and I'll help you practice. Are you game?"

"A chorus line," Abby repeated softly. It wasn't exactly star billing. But Mrs. Fitch was right. It was a start. And any grown-up role was better than what she had been doing. Chorus line, huh?

Abby laughed. "All right. Why not?"

"It's a very important party. Every movie star in Hollywood is going to be there. Some of them are going to entertain, and Pat Perkins is going to be the master of ceremonies. They've written about it in almost every issue of the *Hollywood Citizen News* for the past two weeks. Surely you've read about it."

"Yes, I have," Abby said. "I'd like to be in the chorus line just to go to the party."

Mrs. Fitch's eyes twinkled. "I have more than that in mind," she said. "Being a chorus girl is not exactly all of it. Have you ever seen Pat Perkins on stage?"

"I've seen all of his movies. He's a great comedian."

"Yes, he is," Mrs. Fitch said, "but on stage he has a gimmick which he uses over and over again. He's well-known for choosing a girl from the chorus line and ad-libbing with her to warm up the audience before he goes into his monologue. He picks the kind of girl he thinks he can embarrass, one who'll get flustered by the unexpected attention and the remarks he makes about the size of her bust measurement and her costume—or the lack of it. He cracks jokes at her expense. She simpers and fidgets, and the audience laughs.

"This time," Mrs. Fitch said smugly, "he's going to pick you, and it's going to be different. You're going to stand up to him and match him joke for joke."

Abby was amazed. "You arranged that, too?"

"No. It will be up to you to pull that off."

"But why would he want to pick me?"

"I'll teach you some tricks of the trade," Mrs. Fitch said. "I was very good at subtly attracting attention when I was on stage."

She paused and looked serious. "There's just one problem, and that is you won't get paid. The unions have relaxed their rules, because the benefit's for the USO. Technically, you'll be paid, but you won't see a check. The money will go straight to the benefit."

"I don't mind," Abby said. "I'm glad I can help." She grinned. The more she thought about it, the more excited she became.

Mrs. Fitch handed her a slip of paper. "Here's the address where you're supposed to go to rehearsal tomorrow afternoon. The other girls in the chorus line haven't much of a head start, so you can practice hard and catch up. Right now, we'll work on one way to catch Perkins's eye. Just watch me."

She gave a little wiggle, smoothed down her skirt,

and stood as tall as she could, turning so that she was looking over her right shoulder at Abby. In one smooth motion she rolled her shoulder up and forward, lowered her chin, and winked so gracefully that Abby saw the beautiful woman Mrs. Fitch must have been when she was young. "Try it," Mrs. Fitch said. "Here—stand in front of this mirror and copy what I just did."

Abby tried, but looked so ludicrous that she burst out laughing. "A little overdone," Mrs. Fitch said calmly. "You've got to be subtle."

"I'll practice at home," Abby said. "I want to tell Mama about the job." Impulsively, she hugged Mrs. Fitch. "Thank you for getting it for me. Thanks for your help."

Mrs. Fitch hugged Abby in return, but she didn't smile. She gripped Abby's hand and said, "Don't *ask* your mother if you can take the job. *Tell* her this is what you're going to do. It's time for you to make your own decisions, Abby."

"Don't worry," Abby said. "Mama will be delighted."

But she wasn't.

"Mama, I'm going to be in that big benefit party, *Stars for the USO*," Abby announced.

Mama gasped. "Al didn't tell me! How did you find out?" she demanded.

"Al didn't arrange it. Mrs. Fitch did."

"Well, well," Mama said. "Maybe there's more to her than I thought there was. So much for Mrs. Larkin."

"What does Mrs. Larkin have to do with this?"

"She called three weeks ago to inform me that her precious Linda would be doing a skit in the show with some of the Hollywood kids." Mama smiled smugly. "Now, I'll have something to tell her! She'll have a small part, while you'll solo. You'll be a big hit with your routines, Sweetie, especially if you just put more sparkle into them."

Abby shook her head. "You didn't give me a chance to explain. I won't be doing the old Cookie Baynes routines. I'm going to be in the chorus line."

"The what?"

"The chorus line," Abby repeated.

Mama put her hands up to her cheeks. "You can't! I'd be humiliated!" She clutched Abby's arms so tightly it was painful. "You're a star, Cookie!" she cried. "You can't demote yourself to being a stupid little chorus girl!"

Abby trembled, but she said, "I'm *not* a star. I was when I was a child, but I'm not a child any longer. I've been called a has-been, too, but I'm not a has-been either. I want to get back into movies, Mama, and if I have to start as a chorus girl, then that's all right with me."

"Linda Larkin will be in a skit!"

"I don't care what Linda does! But I do care very much about what I do, and this is what I want to do!"

Mama sighed and groped for a chair. "No matter how badly your foolish, impulsive actions affect me?" she murmured, shading her eyes with her hand.

Abby felt her resolve weakening, but she fought against it, holding her ground. "This is *my* career, Mama. You should be happy for me."

Mama stared up at Abby with tears in her eyes.

"Haven't I always guided your career? Hasn't your welfare always meant more to me than my own? I've devoted my entire life to you."

"Thank you," Abby said. She gripped the back of a chair to keep Mama from noticing that her knees were wobbling. "I appreciate everything you've done. I really do. But this is a decision I have to make on my own. And I'm going to be in that chorus line."

Mama glared at her. "Don't expect *me* to go with you and be publicly humiliated."

"I won't."

"You realize if you commit yourself to this show that you might have to turn down some good *paying* job Al might come up with?"

"I know."

"And that doesn't bother you? You aren't the least bit concerned about the hardship it would inflict on the rest of us?"

"I'm going to be in the USO benefit, Mama," Abby said firmly, "and now I'm going to call Mary Lou and tell her, too. *She's* going to be happy for me."

For the next two weeks Abby worked harder than she ever had before, in order to keep up with the talented dancers in the chorus line. Their dance was choreographed to a conga number, and their costumes consisted of snug red shorts, multicolored, ruffled bras, and matching ruffled trains that fanned behind them. At first, Abby had difficulty with the train on her skirt.

Once she stepped on it so hard she pulled apart the hook that fastened it at the waist. It dropped around her feet and, hopelessly tangled, Abby fell in a heap.

The other chorus girls accepted Abby good-naturedly. Her work rapidly improved, and a few of them complimented her. Abby was delighted when they ran through the number without a hitch, and the director praised them, adding, "Good work, Abby."

But Abby didn't do as well with Mrs. Fitch's "tricks of the trade." The wink didn't suit her. Neither did the slight step forward with the skirt falling away from her leg, which Mrs. Fitch did so skillfully.

"That never failed for me," Mrs. Fitch sighed. "One little movement, and the eyes of every man in the audience would turn in my direction. We're going to have to think of something before the benefit takes place. I know!" She held her head high. "Try tossing your hair—like this."

But on Abby, somehow it wasn't the same.

"You're going to need some clothes that are proper for your age," Mrs. Fitch said. She pulled a handful of ten- and twenty-dollar bills from her purse, counted them, and shoved them into Abby's hand. "There's a hundred dollars there. Go to the better dress department of the Broadway Hollywood and get yourself a couple of nice, dressy dresses. There should be more than enough for the dresses and for a pair of high-heeled shoes and a hat. Take Mary Lou with you. She can give you some advice."

"I can't take your money," Abby protested.

"Yes, you can." Mrs. Fitch nodded vigorously. "It's my investment in you."

Abby bought the clothes, but kept the purchase secret from her mother. Relations between them were bad enough. During the two weeks of rehearsal Mama was distant, stiffening when Abby tried to kiss her good night or good morning. Her occasional comments were usually to disparage Mrs. Fitch or even Mary Lou.

"Why do you want to waste time with someone outside of the movie industry?" Mama asked as Abby finished a telephone conversation with Mary Lou. "She can't do anything for you. You ought to go around with some of the movie kids you know. They could be good contacts."

"Mary Lou's my best friend," Abby said, "probably because she's *not* in movies."

Mama sniffed as she left the room, calling over her shoulder, "Well, at least that boy Luke isn't hanging around here anymore."

Luke! Abby gasped as she realized she had been so wrapped up in the show she had almost put Luke out of her mind. When she thought of Luke, as she did then, she physically ached for him. She'd remember his kisses and the way he had held her, and it was hard to breathe. He'd be coming to L.A. soon, expecting her answer. She didn't want to marry him, but she didn't want to lose him, either. She was going to have to think carefully about what to say to him to make sure he understood that. She didn't want to be forced to choose. But until the show was over, there wasn't time to think of anything else.

*   *   *

Because so many stars were involved in the benefit performance, and because their schedules were so busy and varied, the director never called a complete dress rehearsal from start to finish. But on Saturday, the day before the show, when Abby arrived in costume at the estate where the program would take place, performers from some of the other skits, songs, and dance numbers were milling on the wide terrace.

"Over there—chairs and tables on the lawn," someone was ordering. A woman waving a pencil and paper in the air frantically shouted, "Has *anyone* heard from the caterers?"

Behind her Abby heard a chuckle, and a loud stage whisper. "So this is what Cookie Baynes has come to!"

She turned so fast that the metal hook holding her skirt loosened. Abby squeezed it back into shape as she faced Linda Larkin and her mother. "Yes," she said proudly. "I'm in the conga chorus number."

Mrs. Larkin smiled. "Linda's in the Hollywood Kids skit. Too bad you couldn't be, Cookie, but the skit was cast only with kids who are popular in films now."

"Abby—get into position! We're about ready to go," the chorus-line director called.

Abby picked up the train of her skirt and ran, grateful to get away from the Larkins.

*   *   *

Abby didn't sleep well that night. "Try practicing the wink again," Mrs. Fitch had told her. "I've run out of ideas, and you've got to attract Perkins's attention some way."

"Better sew a new hook on that skirt," one of the girls in the line had said when she saw Abby fumbling with it. "It would be a disaster if it broke during the dance!"

What if the hook broke? What if Pat Perkins didn't notice her? Sometime in the very early morning, when the sky was turning to a pale gray, Abby flopped back against her pillow and smiled. Of course! Why hadn't she thought of it before? Now she knew exactly what she could do to get Pat Perkins to notice her.

As soon as she got up, she carefully sewed a new, firm hook next to the weak one. She didn't want to take any chances with the skirt falling during the dance.

Mrs. Fitch telephoned at noon. "Jiro and I will pick you up a little earlier than we'd planned," she said. "Oh, and before I forget, Abby—break a leg."

"Thanks," Abby told her, well aware that in theater it's bad luck to be wished good luck.

Mary Lou telephoned, too. "You're going to be wonderful," she said. "I wish I could see the show."

Abby's father patted her shoulder and said, "I know you'll do well, honey. I'm proud of you."

"If John Wayne is there, get his autograph for me," Bobby told her.

But Mama became more haughty than ever as Abby prepared to leave for the benefit. Abby took her mother's hands. "Aren't you going to wish me well?" she asked.

Mama pulled away. "My wish is that you don't make too big a fool of yourself," she snapped. Without another word she walked out of the room.

Tears burned behind Abby's eyes, but she blinked rapidly, forcing them away. She was going to do her best, and she wasn't going to let her mother spoil this day for her.

The chorus line was scheduled to perform during the first part of the show. As the girls waited backstage, they heard the enthusiastic laughter and applause given to the opening acts, and smiled at one another. It was a good house.

Their music cue began, and they danced onto the terrace in a swirl of skirts. Abby knew that she performed well. As they ended the number she basked in the wild applause, even though she was aware that a lot of it was for Pat Perkins, who was already running to the center mike.

"Well, well," he said. "And how about all those lovely girls? Have you ever seen so much beauty in one chorus line?"

While the attention was on Perkins, Abby carefully switched the fastening at the waistline of her skirt to the defective hook. She held her breath.

He had taken the hand mike from the stand and was turning toward them. Rapidly he began to scan the line. His glance rested on the blond girl next to Abby.

Abby took a small, hard step backward onto her

train, jerking the skirt at the waist. The hook gave, and her skirt fell down around her ankles.

Some members of the audience laughed, and Perkins's eyes widened. "What's this?" he asked.

Abby lowered her eyes and put her hands to her cheeks, but Perkins, laughing, grabbed her arm and pulled her forward to center stage. "I'd blush, too, if I lost my skirt," he said, and the audience laughed with him.

He looked pointedly at her chest. "Hey, hey, and where did they find you? You look a little skinny in places to be a chorus girl."

A perfect opening! Mrs. Fitch had prepared her for what Perkins might say. "The director hired me because he wanted the chorus line to be a success," Abby said, "not a big bust."

For an instant Perkins was startled, but the audience roared, and he immediately picked up on it.

"How long have you been a chorus girl?"

"Two weeks."

"Only two weeks? You haven't had much experience as a dancer, have you?"

"They told me determination was more important than looks or talent." Abby smiled and fluttered her eyelashes. "It worked for you, didn't it?"

When the laughter finally died down Perkins, his eyes gleaming with delight and mischief, said, "Now just a minute. I've been told I'm very handsome." He pointed to the actor William Powell, who was seated near the terrace. "Just look at his face, and then look at mine.

Both show power, energy, vitality. They show that we're both going places."

"Going places?" Abby paused a split second. "So are a limousine and the Hollywood streetcar."

The roar from the crowd was so thrilling that Abby wanted to laugh herself. Perkins winked at her and squeezed her hand.

When the audience was ready to listen again, Perkins said, "You're a hit today, honey. With all these studio moguls here, you may find some big companies after you."

"Oh, they're after me already," Abby said smoothly. It was an old joke, right out of Rusty Drew's routine. "The gas company, the electric company . . . "

They kept up the banter a few minutes longer. During the final, lengthy burst of applause, Perkins whispered in Abby's ear, "Don't go away, honey. I'll want to talk to you later."

As Perkins waved the chorus offstage, Abby picked up her skirt and ran after them. She was giddy with joy. She wanted to hug everyone in sight, to laugh aloud, to sing at the top of her lungs. But she quietly filed into the dressing room and changed clothes.

One of the girls in the chorus hugged her. "You were so funny!" she said. "You ought to be a comedienne."

After the show, while people were milling around the tables with food and punch, Pat Perkins approached Abby again. "I'm putting together a group of entertainers and a new show and plan to try it out at the San Diego naval air base," he said. "We'll make any changes needed in the script, then take the show to other bases in the United States and overseas. How'd you like to be a part of it?"

Abby could hardly speak. "Me?" she whispered.

He grinned. "You're a natural comic, honey. You've got a great sense of timing, and we played well together. I don't know where you got your material, but it's good. If you want to join my show, I'll get my writers to come up with a couple of skits for us. What do you say?"

"I say yes," Abby answered. She searched the crowd, looking for Mrs. Fitch. She couldn't wait to tell her. Then Abby thought of Mama. She might not react so well to it all. "I'll have to talk it over with my parents, though," she said.

"That's expected," Perkins said. He handed her a card. "Have them call my office. My secretary will fill them in and set things up with your agent, if you have an agent."

Abby tried to appear calm and businesslike, but her happiness was too great. She began to giggle and talk at the same time. "Thank you! It's wonderful! *You're* wonderful!" she babbled. "Oh, thank you, thank you!"

He laughed and put a hand on her shoulder. "Calm down," he said. "It's going to be a lot of hard work."

"I don't mind hard work," Abby said. "I'll have my mother call your office. Today! No, this is Sunday! She'll call tomorrow. Is that all right?"

Perkins grinned. "Just one thing we're forgetting, honey. What's your name?"

"Abby," Abby said promptly.

"You have got a last name, haven't you?"

This is it, Abby thought. *It's time to say good-bye to little Cookie Baynes.*

As she searched her mind for what to tell him, handsome Cary Grant crossed the lawn in front of them.

"Grant," she said quickly to Pat Perkins. "My name is Abby Grant."

12

*M*rs. Fitch was almost as excited as Abby. "You did it!" she said. "And you did it on your own! Your mother is going to be so pleased and so proud of you!"

But Mama was not pleased. As Abby recounted the scene, trying to recall every little detail, she could see her mother's rage building.

"You dropped your skirt?" Mama screeched. "Like some cheap bimbo in vaudeville!"

"It wasn't like that," Abby said. "I told you—"

"I heard what you told me! You want to be a lousy comic. You—Cookie Baynes, who used to be a *star!*" Mama was shaking.

"You want to be a comedienne? What kind? A large-breasted foil for a baggy-pants comic? Or a homely, gravel-voiced character people laugh *at*, not *with*."

"Mama, there's—"

Mama didn't give Abby a chance to talk. "No daughter of mine is going to make a fool of herself like that!"

Abby was determined to be heard. As soon as her mother stopped for breath she said, "Mama, there have been lots of good actresses who've been good at comedy, too, like Carole Lombard, for instance."

Mama's eyes narrowed. "Carole Lombard was never a cheap stand-up comic!"

She suddenly flung herself on the sofa, pulled a handkerchief out of her dress pocket, and began to sob. "As if this weren't bad enough," she moaned. "The final blow was that you gave Pat Perkins a fake name! After all I went through to make the name *Cookie Baynes* famous!"

"You don't understand, Mama," Abby said softly.

"Oh, yes I do!" Mama cried. "I understand only too well. All I've done for you, all my sacrifices, all my hard work, means nothing at all. You're a selfish, ungrateful girl. I've devoted my life to you, and how do you repay me? By denying everything I've done!"

Mama went into such a wild fit of weeping that Coralee, wide-eyed, peeked into the room and Abby's father came running down the stairs. Abby couldn't bear it any longer. She dashed from the house and ran up the hill and sat on the lawn in front of the huge art deco house Carole Lombard had once lived in. Was it foolish to dream that she could be a comedienne as good as Carole Lombard? She put her head on her arms, resting them on her knees. What in the world was she going to do?

Finally, as pinpoint lights from the city below her began to sparkle through the dusk, Abby rose and slowly walked back down the hill toward home.

As she neared the Fitch house, Mrs. Fitch, carrying a flashlight, suddenly stepped into Abby's path. "I caught a glimpse of your face when you walked up the hill," she said. "Something's wrong. Why don't you tell me about it."

Abby shrugged. "Mama's furious. She doesn't want me to accept Mr. Perkins's offer."

Mrs. Fitch gasped. "Turn down a chance like that? Your mother is insane!"

"No." Abby shook her head. "She just doesn't think becoming a comedienne would be right for me. She said women comics are either cheap bimbos or homely women people make fun of. Mama doesn't understand why I won't trust her to do what's right for my career."

Mrs. Fitch grasped Abby's arms and stared intently up at her. "Granted, you had a movie career at one time, but that particular career is over now, isn't it?"

"Yes, I suppose so," Abby said. "But Mama's devoted her whole life to me. I owe her so much." Even though she spoke the words, Abby could hear her mother saying them, and they sounded false and manipulative. "I don't know what to do."

"Ask someone else who has an interest in your career," Mrs. Fitch said. "Talk to your agent. Tell him about the Perkins offer. Unless he's a fool, he'll readily agree that you should accept it. He could be a big help in convincing your mother."

"Yes," Abby said. "Of course he will. I know he will! I'll go to Al's office tomorrow."

Abby couldn't wait until after school the next day to talk to Al. Around eleven, during the five-minute break between classes, she pulled Mary Lou out of the crush of people in the hall and said, "I can't stand it. I don't care if I get into trouble. I'm going to leave school and talk to Al right now."

"I'll cover for you," Mary Lou said. "I'll say that . . . that . . . "

Abby shook her head. "No. I don't want you to be in trouble, too."

Mary Lou smiled. "I'd do anything for you, Abby. I'll even go with you, if you need moral support."

"Thanks," Abby said, "but I'm trying to learn to do things for myself."

The traffic in the hallway began to thin. "Hurry up!" Mary Lou whispered. "Get going!"

Abby strode up Highland to Hollywood Boulevard, crossed the boulevard, and half-walked, half-ran two blocks until she reached the small building in which Al had his office. It had no elevator so she climbed three flights of stairs to the top floor and walked down to the end of the hall, where Al's name was printed in large black letters on the opaque glass window in the door.

She opened the door to an empty waiting room. A few tattered copies of *Collier's* and *Reader's Digest* lay scattered on the end tables and on the faded sofa between them. Angela's reception desk was cluttered, as usual, but her chair was empty. Abby quickly sidestepped the large and dusty Oriental vase, filled with plumes of pampas grass, that decorated the table nearest the door.

Angela was probably taking an early lunch. Maybe Al was out, too. But the door at the far end of the waiting room stood slightly ajar. As Abby approached, she could hear voices, one of them a woman's. Good. Angela was with Al in his office.

But as she reached the doorway, she realized it wasn't Angela she heard. "Lover," a voice was murmuring, "I don't know how I'd keep going on without you." The voice was her mother's! Abby was so stunned she couldn't move.

Al mumbled something, and Mama said, "No, really. My marriage is a farce. Frank is so boring I could go out of my mind. The only thing that saves me is thinking about you and what it's like when we're together." Her voice dropped. "You make me happy, Al. You're the only one in my life who does."

As their voices dropped to affectionate murmurs, Abby was finally able to back away from the doorway. She wished she could blot out everything she'd overheard, but she couldn't. She had to face the truth. Her mother and Al were having an affair! Abby's hands and feet felt like blocks of wood. They moved, but she couldn't feel them.

Backing up, she bumped a hip against the sharp corner of Angela's desk. A part of her mind registered that it hurt, but she didn't even pause. Tears streaming down her face, she blindly stumbled toward the outer door, banging against the end table, knocking over the Oriental vase with a crash.

She dropped her books, scrambled to pick them up, then groped for the doorknob.

"Abby!" The voice behind her was sharp with shock and fear.

Abby rubbed her eyes on her sleeve and faced her mother for one horrifying second. She turned, threw open the door, and ran sobbing down the stairs and out to the sidewalk, where she bumped heedlessly into the people passing by. She ran back toward Highland to the Hollywood Hotel. There'd be taxis there. She couldn't go back to school. She wanted to go home.

By the time she climbed out of the taxi and opened the front door, she was still in shock, but on the surface she was under control.

"Abby? Is that you?" her father's voice called from the library.

"Dad? You're home? At this hour?" Abby walked

into the library. Her father was slumped in an armchair. His face was pasty, and there were beads of sweat on his forehead. His suit coat and vest lay on the floor where they'd been dropped. He didn't rise to greet Abby, and, although he glanced up at her, he didn't seem to notice that she'd been crying. He didn't even ask why she was home when she was supposed to be in school.

Abby dropped to her knees by his chair. "What's wrong, Daddy?" she asked, trying to keep fear from her voice. "Are you sick?"

"Just a little heartburn, I think," he said, and tried unsuccessfully to smile. "I've been feeling it on and off for some time now. Probably, I should pay attention to what your mother tells me and stop eating spicy food."

Abby saw that he was pressing one hand against his chest, and she asked, "Are you having chest pains?"

"Yes," he said. "They're pretty bad. Coralee mixed some baking soda in water for me, but it hasn't helped."

"Daddy," Abby said, stumbling as she got to her feet, "I'm going to call the doctor."

She ran to the phone in the breakfast room. Fumbling through her mother's address book, she finally found the doctor's phone number and dialed it.

Although she was stammering and out of breath, she managed to get past the receptionist to the doctor and poured out her father's symptoms.

"It could be a heart attack," he said. "I'll send an ambulance." He took down the address. "It will probably be at least fifteen minutes before the ambulance can get there, so make your father comfortable. Take off his tie and coat and loosen his shirt. Get him to lie back, keep him quiet, and don't let him know how frightened you are."

Abby hung up and ran back to her father. "Someone's coming to help you, Daddy. They'll be here soon." She gently removed his tie and unbuttoned the collar of his shirt. "Would you like to lie down?"

Her father shook his head, and she saw the tears on his cheeks. "It hurts too much to move," he whispered.

"Then rest against me," Abby said. She put her arms around her father's neck, and pressed her cheek against his.

Abby heard the sound of tires on the drive. "They'll be here any second now," she told her father.

But moments later Mama rushed into the room. Taking in the scene, Mama screamed, "You told him! You had to rush right home and tell him!"

Abby scrambled to her feet. "You're wrong, Mama! Listen to me! Daddy is—"

But Mama was too enraged to listen. "I deserve some happiness in life, don't I?" she screeched. "What business is it of yours what I do? Al cares for me! Al makes me happy!"

"Mama! Be quiet!" Abby took a step toward her mother, arms outstretched as though she could stop her.

"You're always running to me with stories about Bobby, and now you couldn't wait to run to Frank to tattle on me!" Eyes blazing, Mama gripped Abby's wrist and, with all her strength, struck her on the side of her face.

As Abby cried out, Mama shouted, "Nasty little sneak!" and raised her hand again.

"Gladys! What are you doing? Stop!" Dad was on his feet, reaching protectively for Abby, trying to step between them.

The blow, intended for Abby, struck her father on the shoulder. For a moment he stood, swaying, clutching at his chest. Then he crumpled in a heap on the floor.

"Daddy!" Abby screamed and dropped to her knees beside him.

"What do you think you're doing, Frank? Get up!" Mama demanded, but there was fear in her voice.

"Mama, help me! I can't find his pulse!" Abby cried.

Abby's mother dropped to her knees beside her husband. She frantically patted his face and rubbed his hands, saying over and over, "Frank, Frank, come out of it. Talk to me."

Abby slowly sat back on her heels. "Stop it, Mama," she said. "He's dead. Daddy's dead."

Abby's mother looked across at her, white rings of terror encircling the pupils of her eyes. "It's not my fault," she stammered. "He stepped in the way. He must have hit his head when he fell. He had no business interfering. I'm better with the children than he is. He admits it. Why didn't he stay out of it?" She reached out and clutched at Abby's shoulders. "It wasn't my fault!"

"You're hurting me!" Abby cried, trying to pull away.

Mama's voice was low and raspy. "It's *your* fault! If you hadn't made me so furious, it wouldn't have happened! *You're* to blame! You killed your father!"

With all her strength Abby wrenched free of her mother's grasp, staggered to her feet, and ran from the room, away from the sound of her mother's voice.

It was a relief to Abby when she finally heard the siren approaching. She opened the door to the ambulance driver and his assistant and led them into the library.

"You said your father had a heart attack?" the driver asked.

Mama, still on the floor, looked up at them with amazement.

"Yes," Abby said as she stared back at her mother. "My father had a heart attack."

Mama scrambled out of the way of the men, who bent over Frank. She climbed to her feet, breathing rapidly, and gave Abby a brief, conspiratorial glance. "My daughter's right," she said. "My husband had a heart attack. Yes, a heart attack."

The driver got to his feet. "I'm sorry," he said, looking from Mama to Abby. "I'm sorry, but it's too late for us to help him."

Abby nodded.

"Y-you'll tell the doctor it was a heart attack, won't you?" Mama asked.

"It'll be on our report," he said.

"Be sure it is," she said. "It's important."

The driver spoke to Abby. "Better give your mother a couple of aspirins and get her to lie down. She's had a shock and she's a little disoriented. It's not uncommon."

When the ambulance finally pulled away, Mama

took Abby's hand, twining their fingers together as she did when Abby was very young. "You're very clever, Sweetie," she said. "You were smart to call an ambulance and come up with that story about a heart attack."

"It wasn't a story, Mama," Abby said firmly. "Daddy has been sick, but we didn't know it was his heart until today. He *did* have a heart attack. It's true. You have to believe me."

"That's right. We have to believe that." Mama's voice dropped, and she spoke rapidly. "We have to protect ourselves. They'd blame me, of course, even though it was really all your fault."

Abby yanked her hand from her mother's grasp. "Listen to me, Mama! For once in your life, listen!"

She heard the back door open and the rustle and thump of paper bags being put on the table. Mama laid a finger to her lips. "Shhhh," she whispered. "Coralee's come back. I'll tell her what . . . what you said about the heart attack. And I'll tell Bobby. He'll be home soon. And you and I . . . Cookie, you and I will never talk about this day again."

"Mama—" Abby began again, but she stopped herself, seeing the panicked, guilty look in her mother's eyes. For the time, Mama was beyond listening. It was no use.

As Abby turned away, she felt all the strength leave her body, and tears come rushing to her eyes. She made it to her room just in time to collapse on her bed, where the force of her pent-up anger and grief swept over her, and burst out in a wave of miserable sobs.

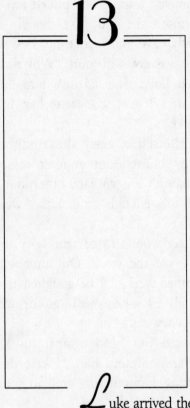

13

*L*uke arrived the day after the funeral, knowing nothing of what had happened. In his navy blues and his short-cropped hair he looked young and vulnerable, as though he were a little boy dressing up, only pretending he was a sailor. Abby, still avoiding her mother, led Luke out to the patio and told him about her father.

"Oh, Abby, I'm so sorry," Luke said and wrapped his arms around her.

Abby wanted so badly to dissolve into the comfort of Luke's arms, but she couldn't, not with what she still had to tell him left unsaid. She pulled away. "Luke, I've kept my promise," she said. "I've thought about marrying you. I really have. But I can't, not now anyway."

His voice was raw with hurt. "Why not, Abby?"

She loved Luke. She *did* love him, but her career had to come first. It was so clear to her. But it wouldn't be clear to Luke.

Steeling herself against the disappointment on his face, Abby blurted out another reason, one he'd accept. "We haven't known each other long enough. We haven't given this enough time. Luke, we're much too young!"

"I'm not too young to be sent away to fight," Luke objected. "We got the word. Our unit will be sent to Frisco in another week. I'll be assigned to a battleship. They won't tell us where we'll go or when we'll be shipping out. They can't."

Abby rested her head against his shoulder and wrapped her arms around him. "Please don't be hurt," she said, fighting a smothering guilt to speak. "Please. I love you too much to hurt you."

"Will you keep on loving me, Abby?" he asked. "When this war is over and I get back, will it be the same between us?"

She looked up into his eyes. "I'll never stop loving you," she said truthfully.

He pulled a small box from his pocket and opened it. Inside was a narrow gold band. "This was going to be your wedding ring," he said. "Will you keep it until I come back?"

"Yes," Abby promised. "I will."

It was hard saying good-bye to Luke, but Abby didn't give in to second thoughts. In the turmoil of the recent days, all her emotions seemed to have dissolved and re-formed again as a strong block of determination. At that moment, it was just what she needed.

After Luke had gone, Abby called her mother and Bobby into the living room. "I have to talk to both of you," she said. "I telephoned Pat Perkins's office and accepted the job he offered me. I'm going to go on tour with him. They're going to mail a release you'll have to sign, Mama."

"I'll have to think about it," Mama said.

Abby's gaze didn't falter. "We need some distance between us," she said to her mother. Her voice was cold, but she couldn't help it. "And I need to find out just how good I am. I may not make it, but I have this chance, and I'm going to take it. I think you understand, Mama."

Her mother glanced at Abby with the same, sly look that she'd used the night that Abby's father had died. "Oh, I know very well what you're trying to tell me," she said.

Abby shivered. Had her mother become so used to living by manipulation and deception that she couldn't believe the simple truth?

"But what about school?" Mama complained. "You're so close to graduation. You're not going to throw that away, too, are you?"

"I have permission to take my final exams early. Don't worry; I'll pass them."

Her mother wouldn't let go. "You said the troupe would be going overseas. That could be dangerous. You could be shot at!"

"Mama," Abby said firmly, "I don't want to discuss it anymore. When the release arrives, I want you to sign it."

She kept her gaze on her mother, until Mama looked away. "All right," she said. "If you don't want me to worry about you or care for your welfare, then that's the way it's going to be. I'll sign it."

Abby turned to her brother. "Bobby," she said, "I'll be here while we're rehearsing, before we go on tour. I know I can leave when we're ready, because Mama loves you very much. She'll take care of you." She paused. "But if you ever need me, I promise I'll come. I'll always be on hand when you need me. Always."

Bobby said, "It's going to be awful having you gone, too, to have no one left but Mama and me."

Mama patted his arm. "Bobby's my good boy," she said. "We'll get along fine."

"Do you need anything, Mama?" Abby asked.

"I'll have Frank's insurance and an annuity from the bank," Mama said. "Of course, it will mean a big difference if you can help financially, Abby. You could have them send your paychecks directly here, couldn't you?"

Abby sighed. "Don't worry, Mama. I'll send you something," she said.

"When's your first show?" Bobby asked.

"In just two weeks," Abby said. She tried a smile. "It means a lot of concentrated work, but I'll be ready."

"I wish we could see it," Bobby said. "I wish Dad could."

In spite of her resolve to be businesslike, tears flooded Abby's eyes. "Oh, Bobby," she murmured. "So do I!"

Pat Perkins and his troupe put on their first show for thousands of sailors in a hangar at the San Diego naval air base. Abby had never seen such a huge audience. The sailors reminded her of Luke, and she realized how much she missed him. "When you come back, Luke," she whispered, "I'll make it all up to you."

The stage director signaled to her to get ready, and she moved to the wings. While she waited for her cue to join Pat Perkins at center stage, her hands felt clammy, and she admitted to herself that she was scared to death. But as she ran on stage to cheers and applause, the fear disappeared.

"Here comes Abby Grant," Perkins said. "Give Abby a big hand!" As she reached the mike, he added, "You look very happy about something."

"Oh, I am!" Abby said. "The sailors here are so friendly. They made me feel right at home. They even entered me in their beauty contest."

"Beauty contest? On a naval base?"

The audience hooted and laughed. As soon as they had calmed down Abby said, "The beauty contest has something to do with ships, I think."

"You mean like Miss Destroyer of 1942? Maybe Miss Battleship or Miss Aircraft Carrier?"

"That's it!" Abby said. "Aircraft Carrier. Or close to it. They called me Miss Flattop." The sailors laughed and cheered again, and Abby forgot everything but the act.

It went well—no, more than that, it was a huge success. Afterward, still intoxicated by all the laughter and applause, Abby leaned against one of the supports backstage to watch the rest of the show.

Perkins's agent stepped up next to her. "You did a great job," he said. "Your timing's perfect, your facial expressions are terrific. You're a natural."

"Thanks." Abby smiled up at him. She knew she'd been good, and she was more sure than ever that she wanted to be a comic actress.

"Have you got an agent?" he asked.

Abby shook her head. Neither she nor Mama had mentioned Al Jerome's name to each other since the day her father had died.

He handed her his card. "Hang onto that," he said. "If you want work in Hollywood after this tour, I feel safe in predicting that you'll get it. The public is going to love you."

Abby clutched the card as though it were made of gold, through the curtain calls, through the party after the show, and through Perkins's speech to the cast, when he told them they'd be doing their next show somewhere in the Pacific.

"It may be a few months before we'll be home again," Perkins said, but Abby didn't care. She had been a success in the show, and she was on her way.

As they got on the bus to return to Los Angeles, Abby took one last look at the cluster of sailors who had come to wave good-bye. A tall boy with dark hair stepped forward and smiled just at her. Abby smiled back. He reminded her of Luke.

Oh, Luke, she thought, *you don't know how much I miss you.* She'd seen his face in the crowds of sailors who'd come to the show, and she'd seen it in her dreams. She shook away a sudden pang of guilt. *You understand why I couldn't marry you, don't you, Luke? I do love you, Luke, I do! But I couldn't turn down this chance. I'd spend the rest of my life wondering what might have been.*

Abby took a taxi home from the studio where the bus dropped the troupe. It was three A.M. when she called Mary Lou to tell her about her success in the show.

"Of course it was fabulous," Mary Lou murmured. Her voice grew stronger as she became more awake. "What did I tell you, Abby? I knew you'd knock their socks off!"

The next morning Abby called Mrs. Fitch with a play-by-play description of the act. She was delighted. "You're on your way now," she said. "The rest is up to you, and I believe with all my heart, Abby, that you're going to be a star."

Abby's only disappointment was her mother's stubborn refusal to be happy for her. Mama sipped coffee the next afternoon while Abby told her briefly about the show.

"I got a great reaction from the audience," Abby said.

Mama put down her cup. "Oh, I don't doubt that for a minute," she said. "I remember from vaudeville days, those dumb blonds who worked with the stand-up comics always got a very noisy reaction from audiences."

Abby clenched her teeth and forced herself to remain calm. In spite of the hurt, resentment, and anger Mama caused her, Abby still loved her mother. She would never forget the moments on the trains, falling asleep with her head in Mama's lap as Mama stroked back her hair and hummed to her, or Mama's laughter and bright smiles as she hugged her and said, "Cookie's my good, my darling little girl."

Abby understood why Mama wanted so much to cling to those times; they'd been happy, secure, nearly carefree. But it was time for her to let go of them, whether or not Mama would—or could.

Abby spoke slowly. "You gave me my start as an actress, Mama, and I'm grateful to you," she said. "We may not have understood each other all the time, but I hope you can understand now that I have to make my own decisions."

Mama just shrugged.

Abby pushed back her chair and smiled. "I can promise you this. There'll be more press clippings about me than you'll be able to fit into stacks and stacks of scrapbooks. Please be proud of me, Mama. Please."

Mama raised her head to look at Abby, and there were tears in her eyes. They reached for each other and clung together for an instant. Never mind that Mama wouldn't give her the reassurance she wanted to hear,

Abby thought. She knew of only one way to change Mama's mind, and that would be to prove herself.

She stood up and brushed back a strand of hair from her eyes. "There's a lot to do before I leave, and errands I have to run," Abby said. "But I'll be back in a few minutes."

Abby drove her father's Chrysler to the Thrifty drugstore, parked, and entered the main door just as two sailors were leaving. As she squeezed past them, one stopped. "Hey, I know you!" he exclaimed.

Startled, Abby stopped and faced him. "Hey!" he repeated, excitement in his voice, "We saw you yesterday—the Pat Perkins show! Down in Dago! You were terrific!" He broke into a grin. "Aren't you Abby Grant?"

About the Author

JOAN LOWERY NIXON is the acclaimed author of more than sixty books for children and young adults. She is a three-time winner of the Mystery Writers of America's Edgar Award and the recipient of many Children's Choice awards. Her other popular books for young adults include *The Other Side of Dark*, *The Kidnapping of Christina Lattimore*, and *The Seance*, as well as the books in the Orphan Train Quartet: *A Family Apart*, *Caught in the Act*, *In the Face of Danger*, and *A Place to Belong*.

Mrs. Nixon and her husband live in Houston, Texas.